In memory of,
Marion and Josephine Narus
Leo and Francis Kosarek

What others have said:

"APPARENT SUICIDE" A Noah Wharton Mystery

Pretty cool. They should make this book into a movie - J.Adkins, Columbus, Ohio

Today's version of a good old fashioned murder-mystery. A real page turner. Thoroughly enjoyed it and look forward to Noah Wharton's next adventure. - Sheery Talbert, Baltimore, Ohio

Excellent mystery. Good story. Had me fooled. Easy reading, a book for the beach. - G.Hayden, N.Y., N.Y.

Terrific! Had me going. Could not figure it out, surprise ending. A fast read. Can't wait for the next book. - P.Bailey, San Diego,CA

"A CRUISE TO DIE FOR" A Liz and Harry Harris Mystery

Loved the characters. My favorite story was "The Game" - R. Nourse, Springfield, OH

Great stories, fast read. Enjoyable! - R. Arnold, N.C.

Very entertaining. Very good. - J. Geschke, O.C., CA

ALICE GOOD

A Noah Wharton Mystery

DON NARUS

ALICE GOOD
A Noah Wharton Mystery
By Don Narus

ISBN 978-0-6152-2120-5
Copyright 2008, Don Narus

Published by
New Albany Books
c/o Don Narus
6788 Winrock Dr., New Albany, Oh 43054

First Edition, 2008

10 9 8 7 6 5 4 3 2 1 0

Narus, Donald J. (Don)
 Alice Good, A Noah Wharton Mystery/ by Don Narus - 1ˢᵗ ed., 1ˢᵗ printing
  1. Mystery/ fiction, 2. Lake Erie, 3. Ship Wrecks, 4. Gold /Sunken
   Treasure, 5. Classic Cars.

Alice Good
By
Don Narus

Acknowledgements:

I would be remiss if I did not mention Lee, my wife and life
partner. Without her prodding, editing, suggestions, and
encouragement, this book and other works would not be possible.
I owe her a lot, but I'm afraid she will have to settle for a big
Thank You.

PROLOG

September 28, 1941

The twenty-seven car Rocky Mountain Rocket, carrying 125 passengers, out of Denver, Colorado, was twenty minutes late pulling into Chicago's Dearborn Street Station. The Great Lakes Limited waited on a siding while the extra baggage car was uncoupled from the Rocket and attached to the Limited.

"Must be something really important"' remarked the fireman, as he and the engineer of the Limited peered out the cab window of the giant steam locomotive.

It was 4:45 PM CST, when the uncoupling and re-coupling was completed. The Limited was now due to arrive in Cleveland at 12:45 AM EST, barring anymore unforeseen delays.

Charles Campbell, dispatcher for the Pennsylvania Railroad, stationed in Toledo, Ohio, smiled as he read the wire just handed him by the telegraph operator. He could not believe his good fortune. The storm that had ravaged the south shore of Lake Erie for most of the day was dying out, but not before it had felled a number of trees across the tracks of the Pennsylvania Line. The Limited would be delayed in Toledo for at least a couple of hours, while crews cleared the tracks.

"Send the message up the line", he instructed the telegraph operator; then he checked his watch. The Limited should get in around 9:55 he calculated, give or take 5 minutes, "a couple of hours would be plenty of time", he thought.

Charles Campbell left the dispatch office and went to a pay phone outside the station. He dialed the number written down on

11

the inside of a match book cover. The number belonged to another pay phone outside a bar on the docks of the Maumi River.

Cliff Ingram picked up the phone on the first ring, "Yell-o". He had been huddled in the booth, braced against the cold wind and rain for the better part of an hour.

"That you Cliff?"

"Yeah it's me. Where in the hell have you been? I been wait'n an hour for chrisake."

"I know, I know. But the Limited was delayed in Chicago." Replied Charlie.

"Any problems?" asked Cliff.

"Actually there's some good news. The storm downed some trees that have to be cleared from the tracks. About a two hour delay for the Limited. Should give us plenty of time."

"Yeah that's real good. So what time will it be gettn' in?"

"Be around 10:00PM. Better be in place, in the yard before then. Smitty with you?"

"He's warming his ass in the bar. We'll be there. By the way, we managed to heist a Dodge panel truck, it should do the job."

"That should be perfect. Any problem with the ship?"

"Nah, capt'n told us to report back at midnight. We told him we bought this car and he said it was okay to load it for the trip to Cleveland, if we did our own loading."

"Good, good. Okay I'll see you later. Remember track five, next to the water tower. Incoming passengers will be allowed to leave the train at the station first. Boarding passengers will be told of the delay and will have to wait in the station. After the passengers leave the train, it will be moved to track five. There's eighteen cars, including the two baggage cars and the caboose. The second baggage car is the one we want, not the one next to the caboose. It'll be marked Burlington Express. There are only two guards. I'll be inside to open the side baggage door, the one facing the water tower. We've got the extra time so no slip ups."

"Yeah, sure. Just hold up your end," grunted Cliff, as he pulled up the collar of his pea coat, trying to ward off the cold.

Charles "Charlie" Campbell, stood tall, he was six foot even, but felt taller. He hung up the receiver without replying. He ran a hand through his thick black hair, slicking it back. Straightened his tie and cinched his belt. He was all smiles, pleased with himself and with the way things were coming together. He had planned this operation carefully, ever since he got wind of the gold shipment. A gold mine in Colorado was shipping two million dollars in gold bullion to a jewelry manufacturing consortium in New York. The gold was to spend the weekend at the Federal Reserve Bank in Cleveland, before going on to the New York Federal Reserve for storage. The mining company hired the Pinkerton Agency to protect the gold while in route. He had just a week to plan the whole operation, but it was destiny. This was the big score. A once in a lifetime opportunity, and things were coming together better then he had hoped. First, his two buddies, Cliff and Smitty got themselves assigned to the 'Alice Good', a lake freighter, with a scheduled stop in Toledo. After unloading cargo, most of the crew would leave the ship in Toledo, only a skeleton crew would sail her to Cleveland. Secondly, the Limited was to make a stop in Toledo for 30 minutes, but no one predicted the storm, now it would lay over for two hours, a perfect setup.

It was a week ago that the three of them, Charlie, Cliff and Smitty were sitting around the kitchen table at Charlie's mothers house, on Clifton Boulevard in Cleveland, drinking beer and plotting the biggest heist of the century. Charlie had just gotten word about the gold at the end of his shift on Saturday. He called his two friends who were in town, between ship assignments.

Cliff Ingram was a licensed Second Mate and had been working lake freighters for ten years. Calvin Smith, "Smitty", was a licensed Assistant Engineer. He too worked the lakes for ten years. Charlie worked for the Baltimore and Ohio for 4 years before switching to the Pennsylvania Railroad six years ago.

The three of them had been close friends since high school, and after graduation they all landed good jobs with great prospects for advancement. But they were restless, they wanted more. Their jobs were not fulfilling. Cliff and Smitty referred to them as "shit jobs". Over a few beers they often fantasized about being rich. None of them were married and none had any serious relationships. Of the three, Charlie was the thinker, the planner. A born leader. Cliff and Smitty were the ever loyal followers. About five years ago they planned and carried out a gas station robbery, just for kicks. To see if they could get away with it. Charlie did the planning. It was exciting. But it almost ended in disaster. Cliff and Charlie did the actual robbery, Smitty drove the getaway car. Smitty was to drop off Cliff and Charlie, then drive around the block and pick them up. The whole thing would take about ten minutes. Smitty saw a police patrol car and panicked. He drove off and left Cliff and Charlie in the lurch. After they robbed the gas station, the two of them had to take a bus. From that day on Charlie assumed command, and Cliff and Smitty followed orders. It must have been the beating Charlie gave Smitty that convinced Cliff not to ask questions.

So Charlie was the planner, and as long as they followed Charlie's plan everything went well. They pulled other jobs and were successful crooks, but the jobs were petty. This gold caper was the real deal. This would put them on easy street. They could retire to some tropical island, live the good life.

The plan was simple enough. The train carrying the gold would make a scheduled stop in Toledo. Charlie as the railroad dispatcher would gain access into the baggage car, dispose of the two Pinkerton guards. Cliff and Smitty would steal a truck, back it up to the baggage car, the three of them would load the gold into the truck, put the truck aboard their ship and sail for Cleveland. A perfect getaway. After the robbery Cliff and Smitty would quit their jobs and get new identities, split up and wait a year for things to cool down. Charlie would continue to work for the railroad. After a year they would recover the gold and live happily ever after. Charlie knew it was a great plan. After all it was his plan.

The Limited pulled into Toledo at exactly 9:55, just as Charlie had calculated. After the passengers got off, the train pulled onto a siding. Track five. The two Pinkerton guards got up at the same time and stretched. One of the guards walked over to the coffee pot while the other laid back down on the cot and picked up a magazine. Both kept their shoulder holsters and 32 caliber revolvers in place. There was a knock on the passageway door. One of the guards, the younger one, put down his coffee and went to the door.

"Yeah. Who is it?" He asked through the door.

"Charles Campbell, Dispatcher."

"Just a minute", the guard unlocked the door and let Charlie in. "What can I do for ya?"

Charlie looked over at the guard on the cot, he was engrossed in his magazine. Then he turned to face the guard at the door. Without a word Charlie reached into his jacket and pulled out a 38 police special, with a silencer, and pumped two shots into the guards chest.

The guard on the cot dropped his magazine when he heard the "Pf-f-f-it, Pf-f-f-it," but before he could react, before he could draw his gun, Charlie pumped two shoots into his chest. The guard slumped back onto the cot, dead.

Charlie went to the sliding side door and pulled it open. Cliff and Smitty were waiting. They backed the panel truck up to the door and with methodical precision the three of them unloaded the bouillon. Moving as fast as they could and without a word, the unloading took less than thirty minutes. Charlie smiled to himself, the original thirty minutes would have been enough time. It was a good plan.

Cilff and Smitty drove off while Charlie closed the cargo door and latched it. He then went to the passageway door, looped a string around the dead bolt, pulled the door shut and tugged on the string, engaging the lock. Clever touch, he thought to himself. With seven minutes left on his lunch hour, Charlie returned to work. He would be off duty at midnight.

The 'Alice Good' got underway at 12:10 AM, they cleared the

harbor buoy at 12:45 AM and turned southeast, heading for Cleveland. The storm that had ravaged the south shore of Lake Erie had subsided, although it was still raining and winds were at 15mph, gusting to 20mph. Seas were running 4 to 6 foot swells. The night was pitch black. The radio operator sent a message at 12:55, giving a weather report and a confirmation that the ship was proceeding on course without incident. It would be the last message the ship would send, 30 minutes later the 'Alice Good' disappeared.

Cliff and Smitty took care of the crew in methodical order, with surgical precision. Two shots took care of the Captain, sleeping in his bunk. One shot silenced the Radio Operator, then Cliff moved on to the Cook and the First Mate, while Smitty took care of the crew below decks. Once the bridge was secure Cliff set the engines at full stop and engaged the anchor wench. Next he went to the chart table and marked the chart with their exact location, then removed the chart, folded it and put it in his pocket.

Smitty was busy below decks opening the sea cocks. Once this was done he went topside to meet Cliff. The two of them met on the cargo deck and proceeded to open the covers securing the cargo holds. One of which contained the panel truck , loaded with the gold bullion. This being done they climbed into one of the two lifeboats, a motorized skiff. They proceeded to lower the boat and when it reached the lake surface, they released the lines, started the motor and pulled away from the sinking ship. It took about two hours for the water to reach the cargo deck, but once it did, with the cargo hatches open, it wasn't long before the Alice Good slipped beneath the surface of Lake Erie and was gone.

Charlie finished his shift at midnight and headed for Lakeside. A resort community on the shores of Lake Erie, south of Toledo.

He had a room at the Lakeside Hotel. It was the end of the season, the Hotel would be closing in another week. A church group of twenty-five were the only other occupants of the 75 room hotel. He got a good rate. It took Charlie an hour and thirty minutes, driving down route 2 , pushing the Studebaker at 60 mph. There was no desk clerk on duty when he arrived. His key was in an envelope with his name on it, laying on the front desk. Room 206, he took his key and went out on the screened in verandah. He sat down in one of the many high back rockers, lit up a cigarette, looked out over the lake and waited. The storm was dying down, the rain had stopped and the wind died down to a gentle breeze. It was still cold and he pulled the collar of his jacket up around his neck.

After three cigarettes and what seemed like an eternity, Charlie snuffed out his cigarette, got up from the rocker and walked down to the water. He walked onto the pier, just beyond the pavilion. He peered out into the black night and out of the corner of his eye he caught the glimpse of a small flashing light. Charlie withdrew a flash light from his jacket and flashed back. With his left hand he reached into his jacket and flicked the safety off his 38, Colt Automatic, and waited.

As the skiff neared, Charlie called down to Cliff, as Smitty steadied the boat against the pier, "Have you got the chart?" "Yeah." Said Cliff, reaching into his jacket extracting the chart and handing it to Charlie. He took the chart, pulled out his 38 and calmly shot Cliff and Smitty. Pf-f-it, Pf-f-it, the 38 spit out two shots.

The events that took place on the pier were witnessed by no one. In the blackness of the night when he got back to his room Charlie was invigorated. He was running on pure adrenaline, his heart was still pumping hard. He washed up, shaved, cleaned his

gun and laid down on the bed, fully clothed. He didn't close his
eyes. At 7:00 AM he went down to breakfast, then checked out
and headed for Cleveland. His shift was over, and he did not have
to report till Monday morning.

Charles Campbell was very sure of himself in the weeks and
months that followed. He took on a air of great confidence. He
speculated with his fellow employees on how the train was robbed,
"they probably got clean away during the storm. Remember how
miserable it was that night."

The Cleveland Plain Dealer and the Cleveland Press gave about
one week of coverage to the disappearance of the Alice Good.
Both papers reported that the ship was lost with all hands during
the storm of September 28. The search for survivors ended five
days after it began. The Coast Guard announced that it believed all
hands went down with the ship. No trace of the ship was found
and it's disappearance would remain a mystery.

The FBI gave up on the gold after three months, although the
case officially remained open for 7 years. What was baffling was
that the baggage car carrying the gold was locked from the inside,
and yet the gold was gone and the two guards were dead.

Thanksgiving came and went, then the announcement came over
the radio on that Sunday afternoon in December, a day that would
live in infamy. "At 7:00 AM Pacific time, without warning, planes
of the Imperial Japanese Navy bombed Pearl Harbor in the
Hawaiian Islands." On December 8th, President Roosevelt
declared war.

Charlie Campbell was at work in the Collinwood Yards, he was
transferred to the Cleveland facility in November, when the official
letter arrived. His mother read it to him over the phone.

19

"Greetings from the President of the United States," it began.

"Charlie what does it mean?" His mother asked.

"It means I got drafted. They drafted me. Shit!"

Charlie was the fifth man. Every fifth man drafted, was drafted into the Navy. After his training at the Great Lakes Naval Station in Milwaukee, Charlie was assigned to a Destroyer in the South Pacific. Charlie's mother went out an bought a little silk flag with a red border and a single blue star in the center of a white field. She hung it in the window of her home, as was the custom. A blue star represented a loved one from the household was in the service, a gold star represented a member of the household who was killed in action.

It was a Tuesday afternoon when Mrs. Campbell received the telegram, "The Navy Department regrets to inform you, that your son, Gunners Mate Charles Campbell was killed in action, in the service of his country."

Two weeks later two men in Navy uniforms visited Mrs. Campbell and presented her with a neatly folded flag and Charlie's personal effects. He was awarded the Navy Cross, for exceptional heroism in combat. He saved three of his gun crew from a burning turret, after it took a direct hit from a Japanese suicide plane.

Alma Campbell packed the medals and flag, together with the rest of Charlie's mementos into a trunk and had it placed in the attic of her home. Then she went out and bought a gold star flag.

CHAPTER 1

I was standing at the head of the stairs, it was driving me crazy. I kept pacing, looking at my watch, jingling my car keys. Monica was packing a picnic basket. All she had to do was pack a couple of sandwiches, a bottle of wine and some fruit. What was the big deal.

"Monica, what's taking so long, we are going to be late."

"Noah please, be patient, just give me a minute."

"It's after 9:00. It will take us at least forty-five minutes to get there."

"Are you worried you will not be the first one to arrive?" She continued to build our sandwiches of turkey breast layered with thin slices of honey baked ham and swiss cheese. With one she used a light seeded rye and the other a dark pumpernickel. When they were about two inches high she sliced them in half and carefully placed them into tupperware containers. Next she wrapped two bottles of cold wine in a towel, one a Zinfedel, the other a Riesling. The towel would hold the chill. Two more tupperware containers, one holding a wedge of sharp cheddar, and a wedge of provolone, the other contained a fresh kosher pickle and slices of tomato. All of this went into the basket, followed by fresh fruit, and topped off with a container holding our desert, two slices of carrot cake, which she baked.

Since I hate plastic utensils, Monica insisted I purchase a picnic basket that carried a place setting for two. Real china, crystal stemware and flatware.

"I would like to get a spot under a tree. It's going to be hot in the sun, and there are a limited number of trees."

We were on our way to the Classic Car Concourse de Elegance. This was held annually on the third Sunday in May, at the Kale Homested Farms, in Bath, Ohio; about twenty-five miles south of Cleveland. The event is co-sponsored by the Historical Society, which is part of the Western Reserve Auto and Aviation Museum and the Classic Car Owners Club.

This year I was entering my 1950 Mercedes Cabriolet "A". I spent three days dusting, waxing and generally cleaning and detailing the Mercedes to the point where I was having second thoughts about driving the car to the event. I was afraid of getting it dirty. There would be some stiff competition and I was in a class that included a superb Rolls Royce, a Bently and a Jaguar. The Jag belonged to long time friend, and all around car nut, Henry Palmer. Hank and I belong to the Great Lakes Region of the Classic Car Owners Club. Hank is very active with the club and holds the office of Vice President. By profession he is President of First National of Lakewood. He and his wife Denise live in Bay Village, a western suburb of Cleveland.

We both like European cars. He leans toward British cars and I favor German cars. The entrants were to arrive a 10:00 AM, with judging to take place at noon, and awards presented at 3:30PM. It was going to be a fun day, picnicking on the grass, swapping car stories with old friends and the opportunity to view some vintage cars seldom seen outside of a museum.

"Okay, I am ready." Said Monica, walking toward me. She was dressed in a loose fitting white cotton blouse, ankle length large print cotton skirt, and white strap sandals. Monica is five foot seven, with a killer figure. Her large eyes and high cheek bones

23

lead many to believe she is a fashion model. She has a dry sense of humor and a fearless, spontaneous attitude toward adventure. In one hand she carried the wicker picnic basket, a wide brim summer hat in the other. Her blond hair was pulled back in a pony tail. She was beautiful. She leaned over and gave me a peck on the cheek and we both descended the circular staircase into the garage.

I purchased this old fire station a year ago and converted it into combination living quarters and garage for my vintage cars. I have in my collection a 1957 Porsche Spyder, like the one driven by famed actor James Dean, a 1950 Mercedes Cabriolet "A", and a 1967 VW Beetle Convertible. The Beetle is currently on loan to Monica. On the second floor of the building I have a two bedroom apartment and office.

My interest and subsequent accumulation of vintage cars came about as a result of my having won the Ohio Lottery. Two and one half years ago I got lucky and won one million dollars in the lottery. I quit my job as a insurance investigator for Great Western Casualty and went though most of the money in eighteen months. Before all the money ran out I acquired the fire station and my small car collection. In my short stint as a jet setter I also met Monica Mueller. We spent two weeks together in St. Moritz, sharing the ski slopes, a villa and a life, I thought. I fell in love with Monica. I thought she felt the same. But one day I woke up and she was gone. As it turned out she was engaged to someone else and meeting me was just confusing her. She returned home and broke off the engagement. A year later we met again in Zurich while I was there on business. We rekindled our relationship. She agreed to move to the states, and for a short time we lived together. A month ago she moved into her own place. We both agreed that we needed a little space and were not ready for marriage. We have an understanding and it seems to be working.

Monica obtained a green card and is currently employed at the Federal Reserve Bank in Cleveland. Her background is in banking, having worked in data processing at the world renowned Gutzwald Bank, in Zurich. She is a computer wiz and heads up one of the data processing departments for the Cleveland Federal Reserve.

It was 10:15 AM when we arrived at Kale Homested, a dozen or so cars were already there, but we got to park near the last available shade tree.

"You see," said Monica, "you have your tree, we are not late, you can stop scowling."

I smiled at her as I maneuvered the car into position. The cars were displayed in a large grassy area with shade trees separating the field from the farm buildings. They were arranged along the perimeter of the field facing the infield. Those that got there early got the shade trees and the shade. Late arrivals got the hot sun. Two of my competition pulled in behind me and got the hot sun, seemed fair.

Once the car was parked, we spread our blanket and picnic fare on the grass under the tree. Hank and Denise, his wife of four years, came over carrying a thermos of bloody mary's and four glasses. They joined us on the blanket. Monica supplied the celery and the ice from the bucket that was chilling our bottle of DeBonnet Zinfedel. We sipped our bloody mary's and breath in the warmth of a picture perfect spring day.

After awhile Hank asked, "Want to go look at the cars?" Directing his question to no one in particular. Monica and Denise looked at each other.

"You guy's go ahead, we'll be along later." Denise replied and Monica nodded her head in agreement.

"Okay, see you later." Hank and I got up and wandered into the infield.

"Did you see the '33 Packard Roadster as you came in, 'ole Ernie put a new top on it over the past winter, looks great."

"Yeah," I replied, "how long has he had that car?"

"Ole Ernie? Forever I think. He's my dad's age. Hell of a guy, has quite the collection."

"Yes I know, he's one of a dying breed. Not too many of the old timers come out anymore."

"Just us wet behind the ears thirty-something's, keep'n the classic thing alive man." Quipped Hank, slightly bent over, arms hanging low snapping his fingers in jive style.

We headed toward a 1948 Lincoln Continental convertible, burgundy with tan leather interior. The same combination as my Mercedes. A couple was hovering around the car, tending to business. The final detailing. The guy wiping down the engine, was approximately six foot, lanky, close crop light hair, a ruddy reddish face, looked very ivy league Irish. A thin, very fair skinned, red head who looked a lot like, Linda Kelsey the actress that played 'Billie' on the old Lou Grant T.V. show, was dusting off the deck lid.

As we approached Hank asked, "Have you met Sean and Mora? They recently joined our chapter having been transplanted here from Milwaukee."

26

"No I haven't, but I think I am about to."

"Sean's with Compusoft." Continued Hank. "Hi Sean," Hank put out his hand. Then he turned to me, "Sean Kilbane, meet Noah Wharton." We shook hands.

"Mora." Sean called over his shoulder. The five foot four red head walked toward us, she wore a oversized white t-shirt that read "Run Jane Run" on the front, above a logo for battered women and a few sponsor names below the logo, a pair of khaki shorts and white sneakers.

"I see you're a runner." I said. It was an observation more than a statement.

"Oh yes. The shirt. I run a little, 5 K mostly." She smiled showing perfect large white teeth to go with the few freckles on the bridge of her nose and the hazel eyes.

"Mora Kilbane meet Noah Wharton." Hank introduced us and we shook hands. "Noah's a member of our chapter, but doesn't make many of the meetings."

"Sean, I understand your with Compusoft. A good friend of mine works there. Mark Richter."

"Oh sure, Mark. He's our eastern regional sales manager. My boss actually. But we only have contact through voice mail, fax or at sales meetings. He travels the eastern half of the country riding shotgun over us territorial managers. Good guy though,"

"I really like your car," I said, as we walked around it. "Have you had it long?"

27

"It used to belong to my dad, I sort of inherited it when he retired and mom said enough of this car business, now they travel. He restored it himself. Took him eight years to complete, used nothing but new old stock parts, no repros. Dad is a nut for detail."

"It's a beauty! You should do well in the judging."

"I hope so. We took a junior at Hershey last year."

"Wow. That's great."

"We've been showing the car for two years now." added Mora.

"Dad never went in for competitive judging. But I figured with all the work he put into it, why not."

"Why not indeed." I replied. "When you get her all cleaned up come on over and join us. We're situated behind the burgundy Mercedes, which is my pride and joy. We'll do lunch."

"Sounds great, see you later." We shook hands. "Oh, can we bring anything?" asked Sean.

"Just your lunch and booze." Quipped Hank, as we waved and continued to walk down the line of cars.

After Hank and I checked out the competition we returned to the gals, who had not moved since we left them. They were perfectly content to lounge on the blanket talking, laughing and sipping their bloody mary's.

"We missed you gals," I settled down on the blanket next to Monica and gave her a light kiss on the cheek, "so we came back."

28

"Yeah I'll bet." piped up Denise.

"We checked out the competition," said Hank, "and I figure it's between Noah and me, or is that I. Noah what do you think?"

"I agree. You don't stand a chance Hank old friend."

"Whoa now, who said anything about second place. Old Henry's Jag will no doubt be the top winner, aye' guarontee it!" Hank predicted.

"Only time will tell my friend. I think this year it's mine, hands down." I countered.

"We'll see, we'll see." Mumbled Hank.

"Do you guy's ever let up?" Sean and Mora had walked over.

"Oh hi," I got up. "Ladies meet Sean and Mora Kilbane.. Sean and Mora this is Monica and Denise." They shook hands all around and I invited them to sit down and join us.

We all got along great. The gals really hit it off, they were all 5 K runners and talked about the different races they ran. We guy's of course talked cars.

"So how do you like Cleveland?" Asked Monica.

"We really like it." answered Mora. "At first we were a little apprehensive with the move, all of our roots are in Milwaukee and I wasn't sure about being able to get a teaching job here. Sean got this promotion so we had no choice, but now that we're here we really like it. I got a job teaching handicapped children, we're

29

making friends and we bought this fix'er upper house."

"A fix'er upper huh. Where abouts?" I was more than mildly interested, Monica and I were in the market for a fix'er upper. We had decided to pool our resources and buy a Tudor or Georgian style house we could renovate, "fix-it and flip-it." Renovation on speculation.

"On Clifton Boulevard, in Lakewood." Answered Sean.

"No kidding Lakewood. Hank and I grew up in Lakewood. Clifton's a great street. How far out are you?" I inquired.

"13930, across from St. Agnes, near Bunts."

"My place is on 117th, between Clifton and Detroit. Small World." I said.

"Yeah you're practically neighbors." Hank added.

"It's a great old house," said Mora. "But we do have a lot of work to do on it. We bought it from an estate at a good price. It was owned by the same family for seventy years. A Mrs. Alma Campbell was the sole occupant for the last fifty years. It's got an interesting history."

"Most of those old houses on Clifton have an interesting history." I offered. "They're all great houses, I'm sure you'll love it."

Clifton Boulevard has a number of Tudor, Georgian, Federal and Greek Revival style homes, with lots of big oak trees. Monica and I had bid for a Tudor on Clifton, but the deal fell through.

"You guy's should come over sometime." Said Mora. It was an open invitation to all of us.

We finished our lunch and it was almost time for the judging to start. Hank and Sean, with their wives tagging along, retreated to their respective cars. Monica and I lounged on the blanket and waited for the Judges.

"What do you think of Sean and Mora?" I asked.

"They are very nice. I enjoy their company. The three of us, Mora , Denise and I have already made a date to have lunch and do a little shopping."

"That was quick. They seem like a very nice couple. I'll bet Sean works his butt off, having Mark Richter for a boss is no easy ride. Mark comes across as being very laid back, but he's tough when it comes to business. His whole family is that way."

"Mora did say that Sean puts in a lot of hours."

"I'll bet. Between work and fixing up the house they probably don't have much of a social life. We'll have to invite them over to the fire station." I always talked as though Monica and I were living together. Fact of the matter is, she spends more time at my place, since she got her own place. Go figure.

"We will exchange numbers before we leave and I will set a date. How are you working this week?" asked Monica.

"I've got a meeting with my dad and the electrician at the Kurtz loft on Tuesday and I'm still trying to run down that pair of chairs they wanted"

During the time we lived together, Monica had been a big factor in nurturing my desire to pursue my avocation. She encouraged me to take a chance when I wasn't sure of myself. She has also become an invaluable asset, working with me on projects. Her input has at times given me an edge. Because of the work I did on the fire station I have become a full time renovator/restorer of old structures. Mostly residential. My dad who is a retired tradesman, agreed to get a bunch of his old pals together whenever I get a job, to do the electrical, plumbing and carpenter work. It's quality craftsmanship at a better than reasonable price. My dad always said I should have been an architect, I wanted to be a lawyer, but I will settle for renovator. It's something I enjoy and frankly I'm good at it.

Right now I needed an edge in the judging of my car. The team of judges, five of them were going over the Mercedes with a fine tooth comb. A white glove treatment, checking all the hidden spaces. "Damn, I didn't see that." I mumbled under my breath. The break pedal pad had come loose and I forgot to put the jack back in the trunk when I cleaned it. Not to mention the fact that I didn't clean the backside of the spare and left the wing nut off the air cleaner and didn't clean the rear seat ashtray or didn't remove my dust cloth from under the drivers seat. Points off, all points off. I wondered how Hank was doing, or for that matter the Rolls and the Bentley.

The judging was over by 2:00 PM and the tabulation had begun. "Well how do you think you did?" Asked Hank. We were standing near the judges table.

"Great!" I lied, of course.

"Me too," he replied and probably lied.

"They sure spent a lot of time on Sean's car."

"Oh yeah! I hadn't noticed," I said. Another lie.

"Won't be long now. Care to make a little wager?" asked Hank.

I knew this was coming, we do it all the time. "Sure why not, but make it easy on yourself."

"How about a Killians Red at Cassidy's, loser buys."

"You're on." I said smiling like I had it in the bag. Hank looked at me wondering what I knew that he didn't.

At 3:15 PM we all headed for the large tent at the far end of the field, where they began to announce the results. In my class, Hank received a First Place. He gave me a thumbs up, then put his thumb to his mouth indicating a drink. I got the message. The Rolls came in second and I took third. I beat out the Bentley, who came in second last year. Sean took first in his class and overall Best of Show. That Lincoln of his is a beauty, he deserved it. We congratulated each other and we exchanged phone numbers with the Kilbanes, promised to call each other soon and it was time to leave.

"This was a fun afternoon." I put my arm around Monica and headed back to the car.

"Yes, it was fun. I am sorry you did not win." Consoled Monica.

"I didn't win first place, but I beat out the Bentley. And that bastard trailered his car. Did you see him sitting in the sun all afternoon sweating, it was great."

Once we reached the road I turned north and headed up old route 21, the top down, a warm breeze blowing over us. I patted the dash with my hand, "You did good." Monica slouched down in her seat and shook her head. I guess women don't understand these things, the bond between man and machine. It's a loving thing, Freud would probably say it had something to do with your mother, or a deprived childhood, but old Sigmund probably never owned a car.

I dropped Monica off at her place, and headed home. It was 9:00PM by the time I cleaned up the car, disconnected the battery and put on the car cover. I popped open a bottle of Red Wolf and checked my machine for messages. My mom called to remind me that she and dad were opening the Lakeside house next weekend, in case Monica and I were interested in coming down. It was her way of telling me that they could use some help. I'd call her tomorrow after I had a chance to talk to Monica.

I picked up the remote and clicked on the TV, I caught the tale end of a story where two divers had uncovered an old wooden boat with two skeletons, in twenty feet of water off Lakeside. The sports was next, the Indians won, it was Novak's third consecutive win and Tofton hit his forth homerun. They were in first place with a four game lead. This may be the year I thought. If this were September this would definitely be the year. I flipped through some more channels settled on a old black and white movie. A Bogart film, titled "The Maltese Falcon". A classic. I finished my beer got another one and watched about half of the movie before my eyes got heavy. All that fresh air, I decided to call it a day.

CHAPTER 2

I was finishing my second cup of coffee and deep into the Monday morning sports page when the phone rang. It was Hank, he wanted to get together at Cassidy's around 4:00PM, to collect on his drink.

"Did you think I was going to leave town?"

"What'ya mean?" asked Hank.

"I mean you're collecting on that drink in a hurry."

"No, no, nothing like that. But it's not a bad idea. You're always leaving town for one thing or another, chasing somebody or looking for some special antique. So which is it?"

"I'm not leaving town, so what's the rush?"

"What's the problem, you don't like my company. Do I have to have a reason?"

"Look Hank forget it. Let's start all over, 4:00 is fine."

"Great, got something to show you."

"Oh yeah, what?"

"When we meet. But it's great. And while we are at it, I will collect on that drink."

"I knew it. It is the drink, right?"

He laughed and hung up the phone without answering. Hank was a character. He and I had a lot in common. We both came from blue collar families. We went to public schools and state colleges. I went to Ohio University, while Hank went to Kent State. I gave up law school after one semester, Hank got himself a MBA in finance from the Weatherhead School at Case Western. Hank was thirty-five, a couple of years older than me. He stood about five foot eleven and weighed a good two hundred pounds. He had a stocky build, his shoulders and upper body were evidence of his earlier college football career. His round face had a perpetual smile on it. Always full of life, never seemed to have a bad day. He did not act like a bank President, at least not around his friends. But then I didn't know many bank Presidents. I only knew one, Hank. Maybe they all acted like Hank. They probably all went to this special school for bank Presidents, taught by Michael Miliken, smile be cheerful, it exudes confidence. Shake hands firmly and don't forget to put one hand on their shoulder when you do, they will gladly give you their money. Bet the school was right next door to the used car salesman school. Ah, I guess that's not fair, Hanks Okay. A nice guy, fun to be around, never seems to take things seriously. Probably could use more like him.

I warmed up my coffee in the microwave and went back to the paper. I finished the sports page and turned back to the front page. There was a story in the lower left hand corner that caught my eye, the dateline was Lakeside, Ohio. Two divers checking out some gear in the chilly waters of Lake Erie off shore at Lakeside found a small wooden boat sunk in twenty feet of water. There were two skeletons in the boat. The Coast Guard was investigating. They were going to try and raise what was left of the boat today, weather permitting. *"That's the same story that was on the tube last night,"*

I thought. "Should bring some excitement to sleepy old Lakeside."

I skimmed through the rest of the paper and hit the shower. It was time to go to work. I had some antique prospecting to do for a client of mine. I got a lead on the items I wanted, supposedly, they were hiding in the corner of an antique shop in Ashland, Ohio. Which is about fifty miles southwest of Cleveland. I had just enough time to conduct my business and be back here for my 4:00 PM meeting with Hank.

Two years ago when most of my lottery winnings were gone I needed to go back to work, but not for my old employer, Great Western Casualty. Not that they would not have me back. When I left the company I was doing specialized investigations. Usually involving large payoffs on claims that were questionable. I had a great success rate and built a solid reputation for myself. So when it was time for me to go back to work, I decided to venture out on my own. Freelancing for a select number of insurance companies handling the same type of claims. Only this time for a percentage of the payoff instead of a salary. It's worked out well and gives me time to pursue my real love. Which is flipping old houses and renovating old buildings. Those built in the 1920's and during the 1930's. Buildings with character. I have a real passion for renovation and restoration. So here I am, 33 years old, a part-time freelance insurance investigator and a full-time frustrated architect, remodeler, renovator, restorer.

As a result of the work I did in renovating my old fire station, I have gotten leads that put me into interesting and lucrative projects. I am currently working on a loft apartment in the old warehouse district located in downtown Cleveland. That's the client that needs a couple of special pieces I hope to find in Ashland.

37

By 2:30PM I got the pieces I needed and headed back to town and over to Cassidy's to meet Hank. He was already there when I arrived in deep discussion with the bartender and current owner of Cassidy's, one Zigmond Coskinovich. Ziggy bought Cassidy's ten years ago, he never changed the name. He never changed anything. People who were unaware of the change in ownership kept coming in expecting to see Sean Cassidy. Sean Cassidy was down in St. Petersburg, basking in the warmth of the Florida sun. Some of the old crowd who ran into him, since his retirement, reported that he never missed the place.

Cassidy's was my old hang out from college days. Wednesdays and Fridays, summers and holidays, it was Cassidy's. Killians Red and darts. We had some good times at Cassidy's, one summer I even played on Cassidy's soft ball team. I still stop in often enough to be recognized and Ziggy calls me by my first name, but with all fairness to Ziggy, it's just not the same. Then again, nothing ever is, is it.

"Hi Hank, hi Zig." I walked up to the bar and swung a leg over the bar stool next to Hank.

"Oh, hi Noah," Hank turned as I sat down.

"Hi Noah," said Ziggy, "what'll it be?"

"Killians, and bring one for him." I gestured at Hank.

"Ah ha. To the Victor go the spoils, as they say." he picked up the bottle Ziggy put down before him and tipped it in my direction.

"To the winner," I said tipping my bottle to him. "Now what's this thing you have to show me?" He took a swig of his beer before reaching into to his inside coat pocket and brought out an

38

envelope.

"Take a look at these, got them in this mornings mail, right before I called you." He spread out a half dozen photos of a vintage black Jaguar sedan. "It's a 1950 Mark V Drop head Coupe. Mint condition, and the guy's asking twenty-five thousand"

"Twenty-five thousand!"

"Yeah it's a steel." He remarked.

"If that car is as good as it looks in these photo's, it's a steal."

"A good ten to twenty K below the market." He offered.

"Why does he want to sell?" I asked.

"You mean why so cheap?"

"Yeah, why?" Is there something wrong with it? Like no motor."

Hank laughed, "no nothing like that. The poor guy is going through a messy divorce, doesn't want his wife to get the benefit of its real value. I mean, well, his loss my gain. What do you think?" He was all smiles and as excited as I've ever seen him.

"Looks very nice, but where are you going to keep it? Last time I looked you were full up. You going to sell something?"

"Hell no, never. Can't part with any of my other beauties. I'll just add on to the barn."

What Hank referred to as 'the barn', was actually a four car garage built of rough sawn cedar with a gambrel roof and located at the rear section of his property, nestled in among some tall pines, not visible from the road. I had helped Hank with the exterior design and the interior layout. Inside 'the barn' there was a loft which served as a game room and entertainment area. Complete with a 1940's soda fountain, that served as the wet bar. He had a couple of slot machines, a pinball machine and a 1946 Wurlitzer model 1015 juke box. The real thing, not a replica. A so called 'bubbler', with colored lights and a full stack of 78's. He also had a big flat screen TV and a dish to go with it. Club meetings were held here several times during the year. The ground floor garage area housed his cars and gas station memorabilia, it was a museum of sorts.

Hank lived in a five bedroom cape cod, in Bay Village, A western Cleveland suburb. The house was situated on a choice wooded lot, north of lake road, overlooking Lake Erie. Hank, Denise and two dogs occupied the house. They had no children. Hank owned four fully restored vintage Jaguars, worth a considerable amount of money. Hank and Denise lived well, not lavishly, but well. I guess being a bank President compensates one rather handsomely.

"Add to the barn? Are you kidding?"

"No why not." He took another swig of his beer and continued to gaze at the photos.

"Where's the car located?" I asked.

"Danville, Ontario, across from Buffalo."

"When are you going to look at it?"

"This weekend, want to come along?"

"Sorry, not this weekend. Got to help the folks open up the Lakeside house. Let me know how this turns out."

"I will, you'll be the second to know." He finished his beer, picked up the photos and carefully put them back into the envelope. I knew he'd buy the damn thing. He was itching to get a new toy. I saw the same thing happen when he bought the 1959 XK-150 Roadster two years ago. Hank's weakness wasn't booze or women, it was cars. I love old cars, I appreciate the craftsmanship of the vintage iron, but I'm not hooked. I don't have the passion Hank does. Probably just as well, I don't have the bucks to feed that kind of passion. Although I still have this itch to get a Porsche 356 Cabriolet. I always wanted one of those, and space is not a problem. My fire station could hold six cars and I've only got four, counting my daily driver, which spends more time parked behind the building than in it.

We hung around Cassidy's long enough to have another Killians, talked some more cars and baseball. I got home a little after six. There was a message on my machine from Monica. She was off to her aerobics class, but I was to call her after 9:00PM.

I called mom told her we would probably be down this weekend, but I hadn't talked to Monica yet. If there was any change I'd call her back.

I picked up a pizza on the way home, it was still hot. I dug out a piece and turned on the Riley Factor on Fox. I also turned on my PC and printed out a floor plan of the Kurtz loft. I've been using a CAD program to help in my renovation designs. While the printer hummed, I ate and watched TV. Later I got out my check book and paid some bills. It was 9:15 when I called Monica.

41

"Hi how was your day?" she asked sounding a little out of breath.

"Just get home?" I asked.

"Yes, still winding down from the class. Mora called before I left for class. She wants us over on Thursday. Is that okay with you?"

"Yeah, sure. I'll pick up a bottle of wine, a nice Moselle. My mom called, wants to know if we'd like to come down to Lakeside this weekend. They're opening the house and looking for a little help. Do you feel up to it?"

"I have to put in a couple of hours Saturday morning. But Sunday is fine."

"We'll do it Sunday, leave in the morning and make a day of it. The place ought to be buzzing, did you see or hear about those divers finding that boat with the two skeletons?"

"Yes I saw that on the news."

"Oh, by the way, I picked up those two chairs for Kurtz today."

"Did you! Wonderful. I am sure they will be pleased." Monica gets excited over antiques. She loves antique shops and estate sales, and has become a very astute buyer. I keep telling her the real bargains are at garage sales.

"I had a couple of beers with Hank this afternoon. He's looking to buy another Jaguar."

"No. Really. He has so many."

"I know, but Hank is like the guy in the Lay's commercial, you know, he just can't have one."

"Very amusing. Listen I'm going to be at the City Bank branch on west 140th and Madison on Wednesday. Do you want to have lunch?"

"Sounds good, how about Millards. Haven't had one of their sticky buns in a long time, and they serve a great lunch." I was smacking my lips. I could just taste those buns.

"Fine, now do not forget, and do not forget about Thursday at the Kilbanes."

"I'm writing it all down as we speak."

"Good. Now I have to go. I need a shower. See you Wednesday, lunch. Bye."

I hung up the phone and got back to the TV, the 10 o'clock news was in progress. They were talking about that boat found near Lakeside. The coast guard had successfully raised it today. They confirmed that there were two skeletons on board. According to the commentator, one of the skeletons had, what appeared to be, a bullet hole in it's skull. The state police forensic team was called in. The boat itself, for the most part was all there, including the transom. The Coast Guard was still puzzled. The commentator continued his narration, "it appears that the boat has been in the water for a very long time. The outboard motor that was attached to the transom was circa 1940. The boat measured sixteen feet in length and resembled a life boat." Film footage showed what was left of the boat being raised out of the water and a Coast

Guardsman wiping away the sea weed and brine off the transom. You could actually read some lettering. Block letters, I-C-E-G-O. The commentator advised that they would up date the story as more information became available. Tune in the 6:00 PM news tomorrow.

A mystery. Sounds interesting. I guess I will tune in at 6:00 PM. I get turned on with a good mystery, and I had to admit that I was intrigued with this story.

Tuesday came and went without incident. The Cleveland Plain Dealer carried a story of the boat in the metro section, with pictures. The state police forensic lab had the skeletons, and as suspected one of the skulls did indeed have a bullet hole in it. This led to all kinds of speculation. The state police would investigate. The transom of the boat was cleaned up thoroughly and it was determined that the lettering spelled out 'Alice Good'. The story continued: Alice Good was the name of a lake freighter that mysteriously disappeared in a storm on September 28, 1941. Presumably with all hands aboard. No survivors were ever found. Nor was the ship ever located. Now it appears that at least two people got off the 'Alice Good', if in fact they were from the 'Alice Good', and if not where did that life boat come from? "I guess we will never know." Concluded the article.

Monica and I had lunch on Wednesday. We discussed our visit to the Kilbanes, and set a time. On Thursday, I picked Monica up at 7:00PM. She has a apartment on West 9th, which is downtown Cleveland. The four story building is called the Chittenden. It was built in the early 1930's, interesting architecture, with high arched windows and carved ornamental sandstone. The first floor is occupied by the "Budapest", a four star Hungarian restaurant.

West 9th is located directly above that section of the city known as the flats. The flats is an area that straddles both sides of the Cuyahoga River. The area makes up the night life and entertainment section of Cleveland. West 9th is not really on the west side. Cleveland is divided by the Cuyahoga River, which separates the city into the east side and the west side. West 9th is downtown. Downtown extends from West 9th to East 14th, north to the lake and south to Carnegie Avenue. Downtown is kind of a neutral zone. People who live either on the west side or the east side hold no interest for each others living space. If you live on the west side you have no interest in what's happening on the east side, and the same goes for the east siders. It's like Buda and Pest. A lot of people live their whole lives east or west without ever venturing to the other side. I live on the west side of Cleveland. Hank and Denise live in Bay Village a western suburb. Sean and Mora live in Lakewood another western suburb. Monica lives downtown and walks ten blocks to work.

I turned the car west onto Superior and headed across the Veterans Memorial Bridge, which was once called the Detroit-Superior Bridge, because once you cross over to the west side, the road becomes Detroit Ave. We headed down Detroit to Lake Road and then onto Clifton.

"The address is 13930." Prompted Monica.

"It'll be on the right, " I instructed, "there's Bunts, should be right here."

The house at 13930 Clifton was an impressive two story smooth white stucco over solid masonry construction, in the Greek Revival style. The walls must be at least a foot thick, the windows were deeply inset. A fortress. It had a clay tile hip roof, a porch that ran across the entire front of the house capped with a pagoda style roof also covered in clay tile, and supported by four smooth columns that were at least two feet in diameter. Two very large oak trees were positioned on either side of the center front walk that divided a spacious lawn. The driveway was to the left of the house. We pulled in behind a XJ-6 Jaguar sedan. Hank was possessed, even his daily driver was a Jag. I on the other hand was quit comfortable with my three year old Jeep Cherokee.

Sean and Mora greeted us at the front door, "Welcome to our home," they said almost in unison. They showed us into the living room where Hank and Denise were seated.

"Hi guys," I spoke first. My stock greeting. Sean offered us each a glass of wine, an island wine, a Matey White Catawba. Mora passed around a tray of assorted cheese, which I immediately commented on as being excellent. Mora told us it was from Milwaukee, and reminded us that Wisconsin was after all the dairy state, where only the best cheese comes from. We all agreed.

When the conversation turned to the up coming Bonnie Bell 5 K run, Sean rescued the guys with an invitation to see his den. A room he was very proud of and anxious for us to see. The ceilings in the house were ten feet high, and the den had this fantastic raised paneling that extended from the floor to a eight inch crown molding at the ceiling. A fireplace dominated one wall, while on the opposite wall were floor to ceiling built-in book shelves. A large mahogany desk sat in the center of the room. Behind the desk were the only two windows in the room. Only they weren't windows, they were a pair of french doors, that led out onto a small side screened in porch. What a great room.

Sean had a great collection of Leroy Nieman prints, which Hank and I both admired. Sean was especially proud of his latest prize, a large chart of Lake Erie. As he unfolded it he told us it was an old navigational chart. He carefully spread it out on the desk. "I thought I would have it framed and hung over the fireplace."

"Great idea," I said.

"Where did you find it?' asked Hank.

"In the attic."

"In the attic? You mean in the attic of this house?" asked Hank.

"Yeah, isn't that wild. I had a collector friend confirm that it is a genuine navigational chart, circa 1940's. Mostly used by lake freighters."

"Man it's in great shape." Commented Hank. I agreed.

"You guy's want a cold Beck's?"

"Sure." I answered for the three of us. Sean had a small executive refrigerator in the room, pretty handy I thought. While he got us the beer, Hank and I continued to study the chart. We both noticed the pencil markings and asked Sean about them.

"I really don't know what they are . I was going to try and remove them, but then I thought, they added a certain charm. I can imagine some old sea captain bent over this chart doing calculations. Anyway I was told that if I tried to remove them I'd probably screw up the chart, most likely discolor, or possibly tear the paper."

"I think you're right. I'd leave them." I said. "It would look great hanging over the fireplace just as it is." I assured him.

"The lake doesn't look that much different." Was Hanks

47

comment when he finally gave up on the chart. "Shoreline looks pretty much the same.," he took a swig of his beer and crashed into one of the comfortable looking chairs near the fireplace, legs stretched out in front of him. "You know Sean, this is a great room. I should have something like this."

"But you wouldn't be able to put your cars in it." I agitated.

"Oh, I'd definitely have it in my barn, no question." Was Hanks retort.

"But of course," I couldn't help laughing.

Sean presented us with our second bottle of Beck's and asked if we wanted a shot of McNaughtons to go with it. Hank and I both said no, so he poured one for himself. We took our beers and drifted back to the living room, where Denise had the floor. All five foot-four, a hundred and ten pounds, she was presiding over the other two women in her best court room style. Giving a dissertation on her latest case. Denise is a public defender and first vice president of the women's league. She defends the indigent, volunteers at soup kitchens and the like. Some of this is new to Monica. European women are not that liberated, but she is learning and Denise is a good teacher.

"Who won Denise?" I asked.

"I did, of course."

"Of course." We all laughed.

"More wine ladies?" Asked Sean.

"I'm okay," replied Denise.

"Me too," echoed Monica.

"Well I'll just have a glass and join you." Sean poured himself a generous helping of the Catawba and sat down besides Mora, who gave him a little look.

It was a very enjoyable evening. We were making new friends. The Klibanes were a neat couple. It was after 11:00PM when we left their house. Monica brought along her little bag, she was staying the night. She did this without warning. But usually on weekends. I didn't complain.

CHAPTER 3

Three weeks to the day we visited the Kilbanes I was awakened at 7:00AM. I don't know how many times the phone chirped before I realized it wasn't a dream. I fumbled for the receiver, my eyes were slits. "Yeah'" I was barely audible.

"Noah, wake up. it's Monica."

"Yeah. Okay. I'm awake, I'm awake. What time is it?"

"Noah, the morning paper, look at the morning paper."

"I'd have to go down stairs to get it, can't you just tell me?"

"It's Sean Kilbane. He was killed last night."

"Oh Christ, no. What happened?" I rubbed my eyes and wiped my face with my hand.

"According to the paper, their house was broken into, he was killed by a burglar."

"Oh wow. I can't believe this." I got out of bed and walked to the kitchen, I needed something to wash the stale taste out of my mouth. I held the cordless phone close to my ear as I fumbled with the orange juice container.

"I thought about calling Mora." She continued. "You know she doesn't have anyone here. They have only been here 10 months. What do you think?"

"Monica I don't know, she probably has her hands full with the police and all."

"Exactly. Noah I'll call you later." She hung up. If I know Monica she's probably calling in sick and on her way over to see Mora.

I drank some orange juice out of the bottle and put a few scoops of coffee in the Mr.Coffee. I turned on the machine and dumped in the water. I shuffled to the bathroom to perform my morning ritual, the three "S's". This was not going to be a good day.

According to the newspaper, Sean apparently interrupted a burglary in progress, he scuffled with the intruder and was killed in the process. Not to many details, the reporter must have gotten the preliminaries just in time to make his deadline. Maybe the morning news would have more. I turned on the TV. The 8 o'clock news was just starting local coverage. Sean's death was the lead story. The TV version was pretty much what was in the paper. He surprised a burglar and was killed in a struggle, with person or person's unknown, the Lakewood police were working on it. More when it's available. Just another homicide, one more statistic. Damn it was cold and impersonal, when you knew the person. Sean was a nice guy, he deserved better.

I turned off the TV and called Hank. His office said he wasn't in. Bankers, I forgot about bankers hours. I called his house, the machine said he wasn't home. Probably on his way to work, *"what do you think Noah? Sounds good to me. Have another cup of coffee. Okay." I often talk to myself, probably comes from living alone. Haven't you ever done that? Maybe I ought to get a dog?*

I had my coffee, waited a few more minutes then dialed the bank. Mr. Palmer would be with me in a moment.

"Hank, Noah."

"Hey did you hear about Sean?" Hank blurted out.

"Yeah, it's why I'm calling."

"Poor bastard. A burglar no less, never figured that area for burglars. I'm glad Denise and I moved out to Bay. You never figure there's a burglar threat, but it can happen anywhere I guess. We're all vulnerable. Hell of a thing. He was a nice guy."

"Yeah, hell of a thing. Think there's something we can do, I mean for Mora, you know." I could hear Hank drumming his desk with a pencil.

"Not a hell of a lot we can do. Be supportive I guess."

"Yeah, I guess you're right. Listen if you think of anything you let me know. You know I'm in, whatever."

"Yeah, okay. Just thought I'd touch base, talk to you later." *There really wasn't a whole lot we could do, I'm sure the police will stay with it.* Mora and Sean's family are probably on their way now. I turned to my 'things to do pad', time to get to work. I had some photos and sketches to study, and some blue prints to pick up later this afternoon.

Monica called about noon, "Noah, I'm here with Mora." *Now why didn't that surprise me.* "She' is really taking this pretty hard. Her mother and father are flying down in the morning, and Sean's parents will be in tomorrow afternoon. I'm going to stay the night with her. Would you come down later, maybe pick up some food?"

I really was not up to it, I'm not very good in a situation like this, but the sound of her voice put me in a position of not being able to refuse her request.

"Sure, I'll be there around 5:00 PM. I'll pick up some Chinese."

"Thanks. So I will see you later." She hung up.

Monica is something else. She'll come to your aid, no questions asked. I mean, Mora and Sean are new friends, we really don't know them that well. I feel shocked and outraged at what has happened. I'm angry that we didn't get to know them better. I feel a loss, and some frustration at not being able to do anything, but it's all a little superficial.

With Monica it's different. She feels deeply. She has an enormous compassion and develops strong relationships quickly. If Monica is your friend, she will go to the wall for you, and she's

52

tough. Tough in the sense that she has resilience and a resolve.

The medical examiner released Sean's body on Monday. The official cause of death: a blow to the head with a heavy object. That object being the trophy he had won for best of show at Kale Farm. The police theorized that Sean came home about 7:00 PM on Thursday. He surprised the perpetrator, the would-be burglar, in his den. They struggled, Sean was hit on the head and killed. They would keep the investigation open but had no leads. None of the neighbors heard or saw anything, even though it was still daylight when all this took place. The side of the house with the den and screened in porch was shielded from their neighbor by a ten foot high privet hedge. The hedge is more than three feet thick and acts like a wall. The alleged burglar entered the house by cutting through the screen and slipping the lock on the french doors. The lock wasn't much, any ten year old could jimmy it. Nothing of value was taken, so Sean must have arrived at about the same time the burglar did. Probably an amateur, got scarred off after he hit Sean.

Mora discovered the body when she got home from aerobics class, at 9:30PM. She and Monica took the class together. Twice a week, Monday's and Thursday's. Monica was the one that got Mora to join, which now gave her a little guilt complex.

It was Mora's second class. When she got home Sean's car was parked in the drive, the house was dark, she figured he was taking a nap. He did that sometimes. Sean was lying on the floor in the middle of the den, the desk lamp and some papers were scattered around. A chair was turned over, the trophy was on the floor next to him. The french doors were wide open. Mora immediately called 911, the police and paramedics were there in less than five minutes. Sean was pronounced DOA at Lakewood hospital.

There was a one day showing, on Tuesday at the Killcoyne Funeral Home. A few of Sean's co-workers came. I got to see my old friend Mark Richter, some of the crowd from the Classic Car Owners Club were there. Hank and Denise, Monica and I, and the parents of both Sean and Mora were there to give Mora support. The funeral was Wednesday following a mass a St. Agnes. After the funeral we all went back to the house for a rather conservative Irish wake. Sean and Mora's parents took care of everything. They were very strong people. With their help I was sure Mora would get through this just fine.

CHAPTER 4

Eighteen days after the funeral I got a call from Mora, she was undecided about going back to Milwaukee, there were still some issues to resolve, before she made that decision. She was wondering if Monica and I could come over that evening. She needed to talk, something was bothering her. She sounded fine over the phone, rational, in control, resolved to her situation. She really caught me by surprise and I agreed.

I picked up Monica about 6:30 PM and headed over to Clifton. It was a warm evening, still plenty of daylight, the sun didn't set until almost 9:00 PM. When we arrived Mora took us out on the screened in porch off the den, It felt a little weird and Monica and I gave each other a little look. It didn't seem to bother Mora. We seated ourselves around a glass topped table, and Mora served some iced tea and that delicious Wisconsin cheese. She wasted no time in getting to the point of our visit.

"Noah, Monica, I don't believe Sean was killed by some burglar." She was serious, there wasn't a quiver in her voice and she looked me right in the eye when she spoke.

I was a little taken back, "what makes you think that?" I put down the piece of cheese I had almost put in my mouth.

"It just doesn't make sense," she said. "Nothing in the house was taken or touched, not even Sean's camera, which was sitting on top of his desk, nothing."

"Mora, I am sure the police are checking everything, it just takes time," Monica offered.

"But the police think it was a burglar. I don't think so. I don't think anybody tried to break in. I don't think anyone did break in."

That was a revelation. "What makes you think no one broke in, beside nothing being missing." I asked after taking a sip of iced tea, to get rid of the dryness in my throat.

"First, the mess in the den. I think it was made to look like a struggle. I think the papers were scattered after Sean was on the floor." Her eyes began to tear, but she fought it back. "When I first entered the room some of those papers were lying on top of Sean. Like they were dropped after he'd been knocked down. And when I was cleaning up I noticed some blood and marks on the floor by the fireplace leading over to where he was laying. No blood was on the rug or the chair that was knocked over. There were no marks on the floor around it, I think there should have been. The rug in the center of the floor, it was neat. Not even a corner turned up. No, if there was a fight that rug would have been

55

roughed up."

"Have you told the police about your suspicions?" I asked.

"Yes. They said that there was an explanation for everything, but right now they were a little jammed up and would get back to me." She let out a little sigh, and slumped, as if to say "yeah, sure".

"So what are you going to do?" Asked Monica.

"Noah, I'd like to hire you. You're a detective, I want you to look into this. To get to the bottom of it. I'm not leaving town or doing anything till I get some answers." The tears finally came. I offered her my handkerchief. Monica put an arm around her shoulders.

"Look Mora, I think I know how you're feeling, but I don't do that kind of detecting. I'm a part-time insurance investigator." I was begging off.

"You're the only people I really know here. I like you guys. I need you guys. There's something wrong here, I can feel it. Monica told me you're a very good investigator, and that you did solve a murder down in Florida." She was pleading her case.

I shot Monica a "you didn't tell her that story" look. She looked back at me with those innocent blues eyes as if the say, "sorry".

"Mora I'd like to help, I truly would, but I don't know if I'm that qualified. You may be better off with someone else, I could recommend someone."

"Noah, I trust you. I don't want to deal with anyone else. I really would appreciate it. Just look into it. If there's nothing there, if I'm over reacting, I promise I'll let it go. Please you've got to help me." *I was trapped.*

"Noah, please, help her." Monica added. *I was really trapped.*

"Look is there anything else? Are you sure nothing is missing?"

"Then you will do it!" Mora's eyes lit up.

I shook my head in the affirmative. "Under one condition. If I find anything I give it to the police to handle." If I do not find anything after a reasonable effort, and I determine there is no evidence to support your suspicions, then it's over."

"Agreed."

"Now have you gone through everything, checked everything?"

"Yes. I believe so. There really wasn't anything missing. I did not go through Sean's desk. I haven't brought myself to do that yet. But his desk was locked, and it's still locked."

"You said you thought there never was a break in, why?"

"We have a flower bed all around this porch, nothing was trampled. And when I got home that night the front door was unlocked. We have one of those thumb latches in the door handle, if you turn the handle from the inside it releases the latch. The thumb latch won't release when you insert the key and unlock it from the outside, you have to turn the handle in the inside. I think who ever was here came and went through the front door."

"If that's true, then Sean would have had to let that person in.

Was he expecting anyone?'

"Not that I can remember, I don't think so." She was trying to think back.

"Was there anyone he hung out with?"

"No not really. He worked a lot, put in a lot of hours. His territory stretched from Toledo to Buffalo and there was some talk about adding Rochester. He spent a lot of time in Buffalo. His trouble spot, he called it. We really didn't know many people outside of work and the car club. You guy's are the closest friends we have, besides Hank and Denise. He did kind of frequent a bar, a place to unwind he said, whenever he had a tough day. But it wasn't like a hang out, I mean he was always home at a reasonable hour, usually before seven."

"What was the name of the bar?" *I had pen and paper in hand, making notes, I could not believe I was doing this. It was second nature. As soon as I was asking questions, I was taking notes, I was investigating, doing my job.*

"Mickey's. Mickey's, in the flats. On Center Street."

"Why Mickey's, why not a bar around here or around his office?"

"He stopped in there one day and found out Mickey, was Mickey Kilbane. Well you know, same name and all, he thought somewhere along the line maybe they were related. As it turns out they weren't. But he kept going there away."

"Mickey's Lighthouse. Mickey's, I know it. Mickey Kilbane was a defensive tackle with the Cleveland Browns. He was an all-

American out of Syracuse, with a promising NFL career, until he blew out his knee. He took his sign up bonus and opened a bar. That was about ten years ago."

"Anything else?"

"No. I don't think so?"

"How about people at work, anyone in particular he talked about?"

"Only his boss, Mark."

"Mark Richter?"

"Yes, didn't you say he was a friend of yours?"

"Mark and I went to school together, high school and college, yeah I know Mark."

"What about the car club, anyone there? Not counting us, or Hank and Denise."

"Only you and Hank. He was friendly with a few of the members, but nothing special. Hank was the one he really got to know, then we met you two. I can't believe we've only known each other a few short weeks. It seems longer." She turned to Monica, "you've really been good to me, and I appreciate it very much." Monica took her hand.

"We are friends Mora, friends look after friends."

"Could I look through some of Sean's things, the desk maybe?" I continued to be the impartial investigator.

"Sure go ahead."

I nodded my head and went into the den. *I remembered* that *night we were all here, Hank, Sean and I.* The room looked the same and somehow it didn't. I walked to the desk, sat in Sean's chair and went to work.

Most people start with the center drawer, when looking through a desk, I start with the top right hand drawer. It was locked. *Can't win them all.* So I went to the center drawer. I found an assortment of pens and pencils, most of which needed sharpening, paper clips, hi-lighters, a couple of old lottery tickets, a return address stamp, staple puller, postage stamps and a Classic Car Owners Club window sticker. *Not much there.* I went back to the right side. The center drawer. I found some plain twenty pound bond paper, and some number 10 envelopes. The bottom right hand drawer yielded some empty file folders. I tried the left side. Top left, some scratch pads, two unused pocket diaries and some unpaid bills. A statement from Avis, a bill from the Illuminating Company, and a statement from BP Oil. Left center was a file drawer, there was no left bottom drawer. There were files set up for business expenses, household expenses, one for monthly diaries, a file for the Classic Car Owners Club, a bank statement file, and a tax file. In the back of the drawer were current telephone directories.

I went through each file, nothing out of the ordinary. I rose from behind the desk and went out on the porch, "Mora, the top right hand drawer of the desk is locked, do you have a key?"

"Yes it's on Sean's key ring with his car keys. I'll get it for you." She got up and left the porch.

"How's she doing?" I asked Monica.

"Fine. She is doing fine, we are just chatting, small talk."

"Good. You don't mind keeping her out here while I finish doing whatever it is I'm doing."

Monica just shrugged, as Mora came back with the keys in her hand. She held them out to me, "it's the small brass one."

"Thanks." I went back into the den and sat behind the desk. I unlocked the drawer and pulled it open. Inside were three bank books, representing three certificates of deposit at the First National Bank of Lakewood. They were dated one week apart, the latest being two weeks ago. I jotted down the dates, amounts and account numbers. I will transfer these notes to a pocket note book when I get home. I like to work writing in a pocket note book. It's handy and I can refer to the notes at any given time. Keeps things straight and my memory fresh.

In addition to the bank books, there was a check book and some pamphlets on scuba diving and a scuba gear catalog. *Curious I thought*, then it struck me. There was nothing else in the drawer. I went through the desk again and didn't find it. I looked around the room and nothing. I went out onto the porch to talk to Mora.

"Find anything?" She asked.

"Yes and no. I found three bank books." I handed them to her. She looked at them with curiosity, like she never saw them before.

"I've never seen these!" She examined them carefully. "Fifteen thousand dollars, where did Sean get all this money?"

"You mean you don't know?" It didn't come out right. I spoke it the way I thought it.

"No, I don't. And that's not like Sean to keep things from me." She nervously handled the books.

"Mora, do you know what happened to the chart. The Lake Erie chart Sean had. He showed it to Hank and I the night we were all here. It's no big thing I'm just curious."

"It should be in his desk. He always kept it in his desk." She said.

"Yeah, I remember him taking it out of the desk to show us, but it's not there now."

"Maybe it's in his briefcase." She added. "He carried it around with him, showed it to everyone, every chance he got. Said he was going to frame it. I don't know, is it important?" She asked.

"Maybe. Probably not. But you said nothing was missing from the house. This may be the only thing that is missing."

"Why should someone break in to steal some old map? It doesn't make sense." She was getting a little hyper.

"Look it's probably nothing. You're right it doesn't make sense." I tried not to get her upset. I didn't have any reason to make a big thing out of it, yet I couldn't let it go.

"He said he found it in the house, do you know where?" She looked concerned.

"I don't mean to dwell on this. As you say, why would

somebody break in to steal an old chart. But the thing is, it is the only thing missing, if it's missing at all. It maybe at some frame shop or in Sean's briefcase, or in his car or at his office. If we find it fine. If we don't, then I want to find out if there is some significance that we are overlooking. I would like to look at where he found it. It doesn't have to be today, maybe some other time. Okay?"

"Sure. Okay."

"How about his business records, appointments, notes, etc. Where did he keep those?"

"All the business stuff he kept in his computer notebook. It's over here." She handed me a leather case. "The calendar on top of the desk is where he left an itinerary for me, so I'd know where he'd be all week."

I stood up, "Look it's getting late. I think we've done enough for one day. I'd like to come back tomorrow and settle that chart thing. What's a good time?"

"Anytime. I'll be home all day."

"Fine. How about 11:00AM, and if you don't mind I'd like to take his computer notebook with me, I'll check it out and return it when I'm finished."

She sniffled and wiped her nose, "Sounds fine, with me."

"And in the meantime you can look in his car and briefcase for the missing chart. Deal." I stuck out my hand.

"Deal." She shook my hand, trying to muster a smile.

It was after ten when Monica and I left the house. We were silent in our thoughts till we reached the Veterans Memorial Bridge. Then we turned toward each other and started to talk at once.

"You first." I said.

"Do you think someone murdered Sean?" She asked.

"I don't know. Mora made some good points, that I can't immediately explain away, but I don't know. There doesn't seem to be an apparent motive. I'll do some digging, if it looks like I'm going nowhere, then that's it. Finished. End."

"Do you thing the chart has anything to do with it?"

"Probably not. I don't know. I was just fishing. On the surface it seems to be the only thing missing, that is if Mora's telling us the truth, and I have no reason to believe she's not. But I don't know the importance of that chart. Maybe it's just my curiosity. Hell I don't know. I'm just grabbing at straws. This whole thing grabbed me by surprise. And how about those bank books, she never saw them. Didn't know about the money, another curiosity. I need more time, more information." I sounded a little frustrated.

"Mora told me Sean had been drinking a lot lately. Like he had something on his mind."

"Maybe it was business." I remember him drinking a little heavy the night we were there, but he didn't seem especially upset about anything.

I dropped Monica off at her place and headed down West 9th,

when I remembered that Mickey Kilbane's place was just around the corner on Center St. I found a place to park on the street and walked over to Mickey's Lighthouse.

CHAPTER 5

For a guy who once played in the NFL, you would think that if he was going to open a bar, it would be a sports bar. Not Mickey. Mickey's Lighthouse was full of nautical things, Great Lakes Memorabilia. A thought struck me, that chart again, Sean said he consulted a collector about the chart, I wonder if Mickey was that collector. It was a light night. Tuesdays usually are. There were two men at the bar and a couple sitting in one of the booths. I saddled up to the bar.

"What'll ya have?" He placed a bar napkin in front of me.

"I'll have a Red Wolf." Seemed appropriate, since the bartender had red hair. I assumed he was Mickey. Besides the red hair, he was big. Maybe 250 lbs, six four, no neck, all shoulders and hands like a first baseman's mitt.

"You're Capt'n Crunch, right? I mean Mickey Kilbane?"

He let out a little laugh, "haven't been called that in along time."

"I'm a fan. Twelve sacks in your rookie year, some kind of a record, wow." I took a sip of the beer.

"That was a long time ago. Don't have many fans today, just regulars." He leaned on the bar and wiped a glass.

"We have a mutual friend, Sean Kilbane."

"Yeah, Sean. Poor bastard. Tough break. I read about it in the paper. Did the cops get anywhere with that?" He set down the glass.
"As far as I know they're still workin' on it. You know how that goes." I took another swig of beer.

"Yeah, ever so slowly. How do you know Sean?" He asked.

"We had a mutual respect for old cars. Actually I wish I had gotten to know him better. Our relationship was short lived."

"Would you like another?" He pointed to the empty bottle.

"Yeah." I moved the empty bottle toward him.

"What brings you here? I mean I don't remember you coming in with Sean." He wiped the bar before setting the fresh bottle in front of me.

"Sean's wife, Mora, asked me to kind of go over some of his things, cleaning up the loose ends, you know. She doesn't have many friends here, so I agreed to help out. She's the one who mentioned your name, and I think Sean did once, indirectly."

"How do you mean?"

"Four of us were over their house one evening, and Sean showed us this old lake chart he found. Said he had an expert look at it. I figured that was you." I took a swig of my beer and watched Mickey's reaction.

"Expert! Well I did look at that chart of his, but I'm no expert. I collect Great Lakes memorabilia, he probably thought that made me an expert. I could see it was an old chart of the type used mostly by lake freighters." He commented with no special reaction.

"Anything special about the chart?" I asked.

"Nah, nothing special." It looked like he was trying to brush off the question.

"Do you remember noticing the pencil markings?" I was trying to bait him.

"Oh yeah, the markings. Some letters and numbers, as I recall. Could have been anything, a course heading, some reference, most anything. I only saw it the one time and didn't spend a whole lot of time with it. Nice piece though. Great condition." He wiped the bar.

"I suppose so." I finished my beer.

"You want another?"

"No that's it, been a long day. Hey thanks for the conversation. I really am a fan." I got up off the stool.

"Anytime ah......"

"Noah. Noah Wharton." We shook hands.

"Anytime Noah. Too bad about our friend Sean, seemed like a

nice guy."

"Incidentally, would that chart be of any value?"

"To a collector, maybe 30, 40 bucks. Why?"

"No reason, just curious. See you around Captn' Crunch." He smiled as I turned to leave.

Not much there, I thought, walking back to my car. He acted a little funny when I asked him about the markings, but I could be over reacting. It was a mild night. Warm with a little intermittent breeze. I took my time and drove home slowly.

I turned on the lights and checked my machine for messages. There were none. I set Sean's computer notebook down on my desk, opened it up and studied it. I turned it on and explored his notes. Most of which were a weekly itineraries, that went back to the first of the year. Dates, times, places of appointments. Notes on customers, notes on sales people. Expense records. I decided to start with January and work forward.

It was 1:30AM, I got through February. I turned off the notebook and sat back thinking. *I thought about my conversation with Mickey. It was what he said about the pencil markings on the chart, it didn't register with me at the time, but he said they could be a course heading. Maybe they were. I opened my little pad and made a note, I'd have to check that out.* The missing chart still bugged me, I could feel myself focusing on it. I had to find out if it was significant, otherwise it was going to sidetrack me.

I thought about tomorrow, my appointment with Mora. I made more notes. *Ask her about Sean's car, did she go though it? Did Sean have a desk at work? How about Sean's briefcase? Did they*

68

have a safe deposit box? And what about those three bank accounts? Where did the money come from?

I closed the pad, but not before I wrote a note reminding me to call Mark Richter. *Maybe Sean....*my thoughts were starting to ramble. It was time for bed. Hell it was after 2:00AM.

CHAPTER 6

Mora answered the door wearing a t-shirt, shorts, and running shoes. She had a towel in one hand and was out of breath.

"Good timing. Just got in. Took a little run," she stepped aside, "come on in."

"Thanks." I entered the house.

"You want some coffee or juice, or do you want to start right in?"

"Thanks anyway but I think I'll just start right in, if that's good with you."

"Sure, follow me." She led me up to the second floor, to a door behind which were some stairs leading up to the third floor attic. She switched on a light as we ascended. At the top of the stairs she pointed to a trunk in the corner.

"In that trunk. It was left here by the previous owner, the real estate people told us the executor of the estate said that we could just pitch it. Which is what we were going to do, but Sean thought the trunk was neat, so he decided to pitch the contents and keep the trunk. That's when he found the chart. Never did pitch anything." She wiped her face with the towel. "If it's okay with you, I'll just leave you here while I go take a shower."

"Sure, go ahead. I'll rummage around then come down when I'm finished."

She turned and went down the stairs. I approached the trunk with the same curiosity and anticipation I have in hunting antiques. There was plenty of light coming from the two dormer windows, as well as the overhead light bulb. I pulled the trunk over to one of the windows and opened it up. I didn't know what to expect or what the contents might tell me about the missing chart. I started right in.

There was a high school letter sweater, some photographs, a pennant, two high school year books, I set them aside. A Navy uniform carefully folded, a flag neatly folded into a triangle and a black leatherette covered rectangular box. I slid the clasp to one side and opened it. It contained the Navy Cross. There was a framed citation that went with the medal. I read it. The sailor's name was Charles Campbell, he was a World War II hero. I rummaged around some more, there was a letter from the Pennsylvania Railroad addressed to Charles Campbell. It was dated November 1, 1941 something about a transfer from Toledo to Cleveland.. I also found a leather covered pocket address book I leafed through it, there were a few names of individuals, some phone numbers, and on the inside of the back cover some numbers that did not look like phone numbers, for some reason they looked familiar, I wondered why. I put the address book in my pocket. There were several photographs, I picked one up, it was a photo of three guys with arms around each other, standing in front of a 1935

70

Ford. The car looked new. I turned the photo over, on the back was written, 'Smitty, Cliff and Me'. I take it the me must have been Charles Campbell. I put the photo back in the trunk.

I didn't resolve the significance of the chart. The stuff in the trunk apparently belonged to Charles Campbell who worked for the railroad and was a war hero. I picked up one of the year books and headed back downstairs, to the kitchen to find Mora but she wasn't there. I looked out through the kitchen window and saw her in the back yard digging up a flower bed. I went out the back door.

"Hi. I guess I'm finished."

She looked up as I approached, "did you find anything?"

"Not much. The stuff in the trunk apparently belonged to a Charles Campbell. There was a citation and medal presented to him posthumously. He was a war hero. But nothing about the chart. So much for my theory."

"What have you got there?" She was referring to the book in my hand.

"Oh this, old high school year book I found it in the trunk. Okay if I take it with me?"

"Sure, be my guest. So where do you go from here?"

"I want to talk to Mark Richter, and if Sean had a desk assigned to him at work, maybe go through it. I'm still looking for a motive. Did you find his brief case?"

"Yes, nothing in it, just some scuba magazines. Some receipts

71

and his cell phone."

"How about his car? I asked.

"Nothing in the glove box, but some gas receipts." She replied, trying to be business like. "Is there anything else you want me to do?"

"No." I thought for a second, "there is one thing. Did you find out about those bank accounts?"

"I checked with the bank. The money's there, as soon as things clear probate it's mine. But I have no idea where it came from. I'm a little concerned that Sean was holding out on me. It's not like him."

"When I talk to Mark I'll ask him if Sean received any bonuses. By the way do you have a safe deposit box?"

"No. Why?" She answered, somewhat guarded.

"No special reason, just thought it might be a place to look. If you had one that is. I'm going to check a couple of things this afternoon, so I'll be in touch. If anything turns up, or if you think of anything, call me."

"Okay." She said, "and you'll call me after you do some checking?"

"Right." I turned and walked down the drive to my car. When I climbed into the seat I realized that I had the little address book in my pocket. I dug it out and looked at the numbers noted in the back of the book. *Why did they look so familiar? Then it struck me, they looked like the numbers that were on the chart. Could it be that they were the same numbers. And if so what the hell were they.* I took out my little note pad and recopied them. As I wrote them down I remembered what Mickey Kilbane said, "they could have been course headings." I think a trip to the library is in order. But first I need to make a call, I picked up my cell phone and punched in Mark Richter's number.

CHAPTER 7

The Cleveland Public Library is a great place for research, and if you happen to be a movie buff, they have a great old film vault. Right now I was into lake charts.

A very helpful lady behind the counter of the General Reference section directed me to the map area. There I obtained a chart for the south shore of Lake Erie. I took it to one of tables and unfolded it. I pulled out my note pad. The numbers I had jotted down were, 83,42,41,36, 1/2MS-R4,AG. Now all I had to do was figure out there meaning.

Course headings? I studied the chart, there was a compass rose printed on the chart. Let me see, 83 degrees would be almost due east. 42 degrees would be northeast, so would 41 degrees, and 36 degrees. East and northeast. *"This doesn't make any sense at all. And what about 1/2MS, what the hell would that be, or the R-4?"*

I was looking at Kelley's Island when I caught sight of it out of the corner of my eye. There to the left of Kelley's Island was a R-7. R-7 was a marker buoy. *"Okay! There must be a R-4."* I searched the chart. *"There it was, R-4, at the southern tip of Gull*

Island."

I was pretty proud of myself. *"Let's see about those compass headings now."* I took a sheet of paper folded it in half and used it as a straight edge. Then using the compass rose printed on the chart I drew a straight line for each course heading. Nothing. *None made any sense. "Can't be." The problem being, I didn't know from where to where. I sat back and thought about it. "Let's see the R-4 is a buoy marker. That much I know. And I know where it's located. How about the 1/2MS. What could that be?" I searched for a MS. Nothing. No MS. "MS, MS, metric scale? 1/2 metric scale? What metric scale?"*

I looked at the chart again, checking all printed markings and scales. Nothing metric. "But maybe it did mean metric. 1/2 the metric scale. Maybe that's it, but what would it measure. Distance? Depth maybe?" Depth markings were all over the chart, but these were in feet or phantoms. I was stumped.

I leaned back in my chair, arched my shoulders a couple of times and rubbed the back of my neck. *"Think Noah, think. You got one of the pieces right Concentrate on the numbers."* I looked at my note pad again. I checked the numbers. I copied them exactly the way they were written in the address book. 83.42 a line drawn under it, then 41.36. I looked again. *"What I saw and what I was reading were two different things. That's 83 point 42, not 83,42. The decimal point!" I looked at the chart again. "It's got to be something on the chart. Something obvious and yet not obvious to a layman."*

It took thirty minutes of concentrated effort but I finally figured it out. Along the edge of the chart were numbers. At every vertical and horizontal line, 41'31", 41'36", etc. Degrees and minutes of longitude and latitude. *"These were grid coordinates. I should have recognized that, it's the same with aeronautical charts, which I know about."*

I drew out the coordinates, they crossed just below the R-4 buoy. Then I measured out the scaled distance between the crossed point of the coordinates and the buoy. It was 1/2 mile. *"Of course, 1/2MS, 1/2 mile south! There was something 1/2 mile south of R-4 in 60 feet of water. But what?"*

I have everything figured out I thought except the AG. The AG was another part of the puzzle. I studied the chart again, concentrating on the area around R-4. Nothing. Then I expanded my search around Kelly's Island and Gull Island. Nothing! *"They have to have some significance. Maybe another nautical term, like R-4. But what kind of naught cal term? Let's see MS stood for miles south, AG might stand for 'A Ground'. Oh yeah, a ground in 60 feet of water, good real good."* *"GOOD! Oh my God, that's probably it. Good, how about 'Alice Good', AG. The mystery Lake Freighter, that was in the news. The chart was circa 1941, could it be that the Captain of the Alice Good wrote out the numbers to pin point where the ship went down? But how did the chart end up with Charles Campbell, war Hero, railroad man?"* Another mystery.

"Maybe Sean figured out the numbers, maybe he told someone and that someone killed him for the chart? But why?" I needed to know more about the Alice Good.

I picked up my stuff, returned the chart and headed for the Newspaper Room. The Cleveland Public Library subscribes to nearly 160 newspapers, but right now I was interested in only one. The Cleveland Plain Dealer. The Plain Dealer from a couple of weeks ago to be exact. Where the story of the Alice Good first appeared. *"Let's see it was the Monday after the Kale Farm meet."*

75

I got a copy and re-read the story. The Alice Good mysteriously disappeared on the night of September 28, 1941, during a storm. Presumably with all hands aboard. Then this skiff shows up with two bodies, actually skeletons, on board. One with a bullet hole in the skull. *"How did it get there?"* It was intriguing to say the least. There was a little more in Tuesday's edition and a little more on Wednesday, but it was pretty much a rehash of Monday.

"Suppose I'm right and I know where the Alice Good is. Suppose Sean figured the same thing out, but maybe Sean figured out more than I did. Maybe there was more to it? What was it about the Alice Good that would cost someone his life? Sean's life?"

The library was getting ready to close. I'd have to come back tomorrow, after I met with Mark Richter. I made arrangements to meet Mark for breakfast at 8:00AM, it was the only time he had free. He was catching a plane at 11:00AM, and would be gone for a week. Before leaving the library I made copies of the lake chart and the Plain Dealer article.

It was raining as I left the library, I would have to make a dash across East 6th, and down Rockwell to the parking garage. As long as I was in the neighborhood I could give Monica a ride home. The Fed was right around the corner from the garage. We could even have dinner together. That Hungarian restaurant in her building would be nice. *Some goulash or stuffed cabbage sounded good or maybe a wiener schnitzel.*

Monica enjoyed my little surprise, we both settled on the wiener schnitzel and after dinner a nice Arabic blend coffee.

"How did it go today?" She asked.

"I saw Mora this morning and checked the trunk in which Sean found the chart. At first I thought I drew a blank, then I came across this little address book." I explained about the numbers and what I had learned at the library.

"Do you really think that the chart Sean had is the chart from that ship?"

"It seems like a good possibility" I replied.

"And you think this has something to do with Sean's death."

"I don't know, but I think the chart is somehow the key. I think Sean figured out what made the chart valuable and he told somebody and that somebody killed him. At least that's my theory."

"Have you any idea what makes the chart valuable?" She asked.

"No. But I'm going back to the library tomorrow. I have to find out more about that ship."

"Suppose you solve the puzzle, and you figure out what makes the chart valuable. Then what?"

"Well it would provide a motive. Then we have to find out who else knew. And just maybe that someone is the killer."

"Just remember the condition you put on this investigation." She reminded me. "Whatever you find out you will take to the police." I was being put on notice. "You will not do anything foolish." I was being warned.

"Are you worried?" I smiled.

"Yes I am. You have a tendency to get carried away." She was not smiling. "If Sean was murdered, this is serious. It is nothing to fool around with. You could be in danger." She was very serious.

I took her hand, "Look, don't worry. I promise I won't go off chasing bad guy's. Besides, it's not my style."

"Would you like to come upstairs. We could pop some corn, maybe watch a movie."

Her invitation was tempting but I turned it down. "I've got an early appointment with Mark Richter." She looked a little disappointed. We parted with a kiss at the elevator. "I'll call you tomorrow." The elevator doors were closing.

CHAPTER 8

I arrived at Denny's, on Rockside Road ten minutes early. The waitress topped off my coffee for the second time when Mark entered the restaurant. He was carrying a box, about one foot square. Looking around the restaurant he finally spotted me, smiled and walked over.

Mark Richter stood six feet tall, blond, blue eyed, square jaw. He wore a dark blue blazer over a pair of Bills Khakis, with a blue button down shirt and pull on soft loafers. He looked like one of those models in a J.Crew catalog. Mark and I were best friends all through high school and college. After college we drifted in different directions. We are still friends, but no longer hang out together.

I stood up as he approached. We shook hands and he slid into the booth, pushing the box ahead of him. As soon as he was seated a waitress came over.

"How about some breakfast?" I asked.

"Just coffee, thanks." He put the box on the table.

The waitress smiled at Mark as she took the order. Mark smiled back. Mark is a typical, womanizing, male chauvinist and hits on every female over 18 years of age. He is proud of his reputation and wares it like a badge of distinction. It's actually part of his charm, his persona.

"So you're detecting again." I did some investigating for Mark and his sister some time back, but that's another story.

"Not really. I'm checking into a couple of things for Mora Kilbane, but nothing sinister. She's just trying to tie up a few loose ends."

"Right." He sat back in the booth, playing with his coffee cup. "So how can I help?"

"For openers, was Sean paid any bonuses in the last few weeks?"

"No. CompuSoft doesn't have a bonus program. Why?" He asked.

"Well, Mora found some money, actually some bank deposits

79

that she could not account for." I took a sip of my coffee. It was cooling off. I signaled the waitress.

"Well it didn't come from CompuSoft. Sean was paid a salary and commission, nothing more."

"I see," it didn't look like this conversation was going anywhere. The waitress arrived to refresh our cups.

"Incidentally," Mark put his hand on the box he brought, "I had Sean's desk cleaned out. His stuff is in the box."

"Oh." I looked at the box. Apparently Mark was one step ahead of me.

"I just assumed from our phone conversation, that it would be okay to bring it."

"That's fine. I'll see that Mora gets it." I put my hand on the box and slid it to my side of the table. "What did you think of Sean? Personally and as an employee?"

"Sean was a good salesman. And, he had the makings of a good territorial manager. He was conscientious, personable, always did his homework. Personally, I didn't know him all that well. He seemed like a nice guy. We had a couple of beers, but I never really got to know him outside the company." He took a sip of his coffee and made a face. "Cold. Where's that waitress." He looked around and finally got her attention. He motioned to her and pointed to his cup. She nodded and came right over with hot coffee, in a fresh cup. For Mark, not for me.

"What do you mean, the makings of a good territorial manager. I thought that's what he was?"

"He was." He took the cup from the waitress and handed her his cold cup. "Thanks." Another exchange of smiles. "I just meant that he had a lot to learn, to become a good one. For example: He spent to much time in Buffalo, like three visits in the last five weeks."

"Mora told me Buffalo was a problem area for Sean."

"Hell no! Buffalo was a gift. That place runs on autopilot. The salesman for Buffalo is one hump'n puppy, a real producer. A visit there once every six weeks would have been sufficient. Now Toledo, that was another story. He should have spent more time in Toledo. That's what I meant by having more to learn." He drank some of his hot coffee.

"Had you talked to him about that?" I asked.

"Yeah I did. He just agreed with me and that was it. Not enough time to see any changes."

"This was recent?" I asked.

"Week before he was killed. Poor bastard."

My coffee was ice cold. Mark motioned to the waitress and pointed to my cup. She nodded and came right over with a pot of fresh coffee and filled my cup. No fresh cup for me. I looked at the waitress, who was smiling at Mark. "Thanks." The waitress continued to look at Mark as she left the table. "Mark, did Sean ever mention an old Lake Erie chart he found?"

"No. Why?"

"Nothing special. It's just that he found this old chart and according to Mora, was very excited and was telling everyone who would listen. I just thought, maybe ......"

"Nope. Didn't say anything to me."

I changed the subject, "So where are you off to this morning?"

"Atlanta."

"Atlanta!"

"Yeah. Sales meeting. They keep me hopping."

"The price of fame and fortune." I pushed my coffee cup to the side. I'd had enough.

"Ah yes." He looked at his watch. "Listen, I've got to run, but if there's anything else, let me know. I really would like to help anyway I can." He pushed the coffee away and put both hands on the table.

"Hey, thanks for bringing Sean's stuff. Give my regards to the rest of the family. It's been awhile."

"No problem," he got up to leave, "Sorry I have to run like this."

We shook hands. "Keep in touch." He said.

"Right." I replied. We were still friends, but somehow things were different. Then again we all change. Change between friends is always gradual. Neither one is aware, it just happens. When we finally recognize it, we contemplate the change and move on.

We're still friends, just different.

It was 9:30, I pulled out my cell phone and called Mora. I told her about my meeting with Mark and the box of Sean's stuff. I told her I would drop it off later. I also told her I thought I had figured out what the chart was, at least part of it, but I had a little more work to do. She told me Mickey Kilbane had called her and offered to buy the chart."

"Really!"

"Yes, he called last night, said he wouldn't mind having it for his collection. He expressed his sympathy and said that he hoped he wasn't upsetting me or anything. He said you had mentioned the chart to him."

"Well I did stop in to see him, and I did ask him about the chart. But I didn't say it was for sale. What did you say to him?"

"I thanked him for calling, and told him I would consider his offer."

"Good. You did the right thing. I need to do more checking, then I'll stop in and talk to him again. Hopefully by then I'll have more information on the chart. So, I'll talk to you later." *Now that was a little curious. Mickey Kilbane's sudden interest in the chart.* I called my answering machine and retrieved my messages. My dad called to remind me we were meeting Kurtz at the loft, tomorrow morning at 10:00. Monica called to remind me of the Kurtz meeting. "Like they think I'll forget." Hank called, he wanted me to come over this afternoon and see his new toy. I returned Hank's call.

"So you went ahead and bought the car. Why didn't you tell me,

I would have helped you bring it home."

"No need, all taken care of. Actually I've had the car for a couple of weeks. It's been in the shop getting a full detail treatment. But it's home now and I'd like you to see it. A thing of beauty, I assure you."

"Watch it, you're salivating all over the phone."

"Opp's, sorry. Will you be able to come over or do I have to drag you?" He was insistent.

"I'll be tied up for a few hours, how about later this afternoon, say around four or five."

"Perfect. The pussycat and I will be waiting. Pussycat, get it. Jaguar, pussycat. A Jaguar is a big pussycat."

I was silent for a few seconds, "Oh yeah, pussycat. Now I get it. Pussycat, Jaguar, oh, yeah."

"Screw you Wharton. I'll see you later." He hung up.

I let out a laugh. I love playing with Hank's head. He was an easy put on. I drove downtown, back to the library.

CHAPTER 9

All of the newspaper information I was looking for was on
micro film. The Librarian brought me several boxes, covering a
two week period beginning with September 28, 1941. At the time
there were three daily newspapers in town. The Cleveland Plain
Dealer, The Cleveland Press and the The Cleveland News. I
started with the Plain Dealer, since that paper was still around. On
September 29th they carried a story with photos, showing the Alice
Good in earlier days.

The Alice Good was a dry cargo vessel. Which meant just that.
She carried dry cargo as opposed to liquid. No coal or limestone
either, like most of the Great Lakes carriers. She was 250 foot in
length. Weighed 1900 tons. Not a very big ship, but very
serviceable and suitable for her duties on the lakes. Her keel was
laid down in 1925, by the Carlson Ship Building Company, of Port
Huron, Michigan. She was launched in 1926, as a coal burning
steamship. She was later converted to diesel in 1938. She had a
great record without mishaps. The original Captain Ira Davenport,
retired in 1939. Captain Damon Clark assumed command after
Davenport. The ship managed to weather most storms without
incident and carried a normal compliment of 15 crew members,
including the Captain.

On the night of September 28, 1941, the Alice Good sailed out
of Toledo bound for Cleveland with a skeleton crew and no cargo.
She was to take on cargo in Cleveland, along with the balance of a
crew and sail to Buffalo. A storm had been blowing all that day,
the seas at times were heavy. Once out of port and when they
cleared the Toledo channel, the radioman sent a message, that all
was well. Then the Alice Good just disappeared without a trace.

It was presumed that all crew members went down with the ship. There was a list of crew members: Captain Clark, 2nd Mate: Clifford Igram, Wheelman: Tony Wells, Radioman: Henry Wycoski, Maintenance Man: Oliver Richards, Oiler: Richard Tweeks, 1st Assistant Engineer: Calvin Smith, Chief Engineer: Wendal Adams. All were experienced sailors, except Oliver Richards, he was eighteen years old and this was his first voyage. He was carried as a Maintenance Man, but was actually an apprentice seaman.

"The ship was empty and eight men died. Not much of a motive for stealing the chart. If in fact the chart in question was from the Alice Good." There were two big stories on page one of all three papers. In addition to the mysterious disappearance of the Alice Good, there was a train robbery. A big one. Over two million dollars in gold bullion was heisted from the Great Lakes Limited. The gold was carried in a special baggage car guarded by two Pinkerton agents. When the train arrived in Cleveland, authorities had to force open the door to the baggage car, which was locked from the inside. They found the two guards dead and the gold gone. It was baffling and presented a real puzzle for the authorities. The FBI deduced that the gold was removed from the train in Toledo, during its two hour lay over.

The FBI had no answer for the door being locked from the inside. There were no suspects. A drag net had been launched. The Police and FBI calculated that you would need a truck to move that much gold, fifty wood boxes in all. A total weight of nearly 1600 pounds. They also determined that there had to be more than one man involved.

During the days and weeks that followed nothing turned up, soon the story faded away. I sat there contemplating all this. It was interesting. Charles Campbell, the Navy hero, who's trunk was in Sean and Mora's attic, worked for the railroad at the time of the robbery. If my memory serves me, I dug out my little note pad and doubled checked, he was the dispatcher for the Pennsylvania Railroad in Toledo. I dug into my portfolio for the old address book I took from the attic. I paged through it, nothing but names. addresses and phone numbers, what you would expect. It was the names that struck me. Two names in particular. Cliff Ingram and Smitty. I made copies of all the stories, from each paper. This amounted to three weeks of stories.

It was almost 2:30PM when I left the library, time enough for a quick lunch and a return visit to Mickey's Lighthouse. I pulled into Mickey's lot and waited while a car backed out, then I maneuvered the Cherokee into the same parking space. It was a very warm afternoon, The air conditioning felt good as I entered the premises.

I took a seat at the bar. The barmaid came over, "What'll it be?" She asked, as she wiped the area in front of me and deposited a cocktail napkin.

"I'll have a draft and I'd like to see the sandwich menu." She returned with a frosty mug and the menu. I took a slug of the beer, which tasted great, and looked at the menu.
The barmaid waited while I decided.

"The pastrami on rye, mustard and a pickle on the side." She nodded without a word and retrieved the menu. I looked around but didn't see Mickey. The sandwich arrived a few minutes later. "I'll have a refill", I pointed to the empty glass, "is Mickey around?"

"No, doesn't come in till 5:00. Anything else?" She set the refilled glass on the cocktail napkin.

"Nope, that's it." I bit down on the sandwich. Not bad. I imagine Mickey does a nice lunch trade, the bar was still pretty empty. I noticed the sign on the back bar, "Cocktail Hour 4:30 to 6:30, Hot Hors d'oeuvres" I hung around killing time. The barmaid was not very talkative, she didn't much like answering any questions, maybe because they all concerned her boss. After awhile I decided I was getting nowhere. *I think I'll go see Hank then come back.*

The drive out to Hank's place took about 35 minutes. I saw his Jag parked in the drive, I assumed he was home. I parked behind his car and walked out back to the barn.

"Hello! Anyone home?"

"Hi Noah." The garage door was open and Hank was wiping down his new toy. "Come on over and take a look." He stopped wiping the windshield and stood back to admire his treasure.

"Wow! Some car. Sure is a beauty." I walked around the car admiring the fine lines. "Looks like you did a number on it." I looked inside, "did you redo the upholstery?"

"Nope. That's all original." He stood there proudly.

"You're kidding. Doesn't look sat on. Absolutely no wear. What's the mileage?"

"She's showing 39,000 and that's been authenticated."

"What all did you do to it?"

88

"Basically a good clean-up and some minor paint work. The tires and exhaust are recent replacements. Brakes have little wear." He leaned inside and released the hood latch.

"What did you say you paid for this?"

"Well I told you the asking price was twenty-five K, I made him a cash offer of twenty-three K and he took it." Hank had this big smile on his face. "That's twenty-three K US, which translates to thirty-five+ Canadian. I was happy, he was happy."

"Did you take a gun with you, I mean you stole it. Fantastic car, these old Mark V Dropheads are classy looking cars. Look at that burl wood dash and the window sill moldings, and the leather, just outstanding." I was very impressed.

"Go ahead sit in it. Try it out." I accepted his invitation and sat behind the wheel. The old Jag's are every bit as nice as the old Mercedes, but I would never admit that to Hank.
"What a beauty," I fondled the steering wheel.

"Want to take it for a spin?"

"Sure, but you drive." I slid out from behind the wheel.

"I love it, let me give the oil a check first." He raised the hood and propped it open.

The engine was immaculate. This car was a real steal. I don't know how he finds these cars. It's the second one in like condition that he's come up with. Absolutely amazing. Hank closed the hood and went around to the drivers side. I opened the passenger door and slid in. When he fired up the car you could barely hear the motor running. When he stepped on the gas, it let out a low muffled roar.

"What a sweet sound." Hank was in his glory.

We cruised around for about an hour before heading back to his barn. The car's performance was flawless. I marveled at the quiet of this beautiful car, "pure luxury". When we returned, Hank parked the car inside his barn. I noticed he moved the other cars a little closer to each other and made room for the coupe.

"Come on up and have a beer," Hank said, as he walked toward the stairs leading up to the loft.

"Right behind you."

Hank went over to a modified Pepsi vending machine, opened it and removed two bottles of Sam Adams. The idea for modifying the vending machine came from me. I did the same to a fifties coke machine. Only mine still dispenses bottled coke in addition to keeping my beer cold.

"Hey will you excuse me for a minute," he looked at his watch, "I promised to call this guy."

"Sure, go ahead." I made myself comfortable in one of two leather arm chairs.

Hank picked up the phone and dialed, then he began talking, "Lake Road", pause, "Heading toward Cleveland", pause, "That's right", pause, "Good." The call didn't take long. Hank came over and sat down in the other arm chair.

"So Noah what's happening with your investigation?" He raised his bottle and took a swig of beer.

"What investigation is that?" I asked, a little puzzled at the question, then I realized that Denise was Mora's attorney.

"Mora told us you were looking into the burglary. How's it going?"

"Mora doesn't believe it was a burglary. She thinks Sean was murdered." I let the statement sink in. At least I thought I was letting it sink in.

"Yeah, I know. I told her she was grabbing at straws. She ought to let the police do their thing. Don't you agree?"

"I didn't make her any promises. She has some valid points, but I don't see a motive. Anyway I promised to look around, if nothing comes up then that's it. What do you think?"

"I think she's way off base. I know it's hard on her, I understand that, but I think she's trying to turn nothing into something. She just doesn't want to accept what it is. Sean was killed and that's it. She should let it go and move on." He finished his beer and went to the machine for another. "You want one?" He asked.

"No, I'm okay."

"So, what do you think?" He asked.

"I honestly don't know what to think. There are a couple of loose ends, like three bank accounts Mora knew nothing about."

"Yeah she asked me about those. I mean since they are with my bank."

"And, what about them?" I asked.

"I don't know, The money's there. It's all legit. Maybe he won the lottery, like someone else I know." He smiled at me.

"Really, you think there's some simple explanation."

"Yes I do." He said.

"Why didn't he tell Mora?" I finished my beer and set the bottle down on the floor next to the chair.

"Hell I don't know, I don't tell Denise everything. Maybe it was supposed to be a surprise or something. I don't see it as any big thing. I mean if that's all there is, com'on."

"Yeah, but it's still a loose end." I got up.

"You ready for another beer, help yourself." He gestured over to the Pepsi machine.

"Thanks, maybe just one more, than I gotta get going."

"So you really like my car." He tried to change the subject.

"Yes I do." I paused, "You know the chart Sean showed us that night at his house. Well it's missing."

"Really. Is that another loose end or something?" It was the way he said it. Making the whole thing sound a little silly.

"It is a loose end." I was defending my statement and at the same time I was sounding a little foolish, I was getting pissed. Maybe Hank was right. "Look it's the only thing that came up missing from the so called burglary."

"Hell maybe he sent it out to have it framed. Didn't he say that's what he wanted to do? Have it framed." Hank was right, it is what Sean said that night. Why didn't I pursue that. Maybe he did send it out, maybe it's sitting in some frame shop. Maybe I am being a little foolish, it sure felt that way. "Yeah you're probably right." It's all I could say.

"Noah I'm not trying to rain on your parade. I'm sure you know what you're doing, and I'm sure you have honorable motives, but a couple of bank accounts and an old map. Isn't that just a little thin. Between you and me, I think Mora is just a little paranoid." He swigged his beer. "Maybe that cute little body of hers has got you a bit confused 'ole buddy." He gave me a little smile and winked.

"Hank you're way off base." I stood up, it was time to leave, he was getting on my nerves.

He held up his hands, "hey, okay. I didn't mean anything. Just forget it. Have another beer." He stood up with me.

"No, I think it's time to go."

"Suit yourself. Look I'm sorry. I got out of line. Probably the beer. Okay." He held out his hand.

"Sure. Okay." We shook hands and I left.

Walking back to my car I noticed Denise through the kitchen window. She must have gotten home while we were in the barn I figured I better stop and say hello or she'd be pissed. So I did. We made small talk while Hank was in the barn putting away his toys. Ten minutes later I was on my way.

Out of the drive I thought about what Hank had said. *He might be right, maybe the chart was being framed. Maybe there was a perfectly simple explanation for the bank accounts, maybe it was a botched burglary after all. Still there were the things Mora said about that night that gave me cause for doubt. She did make a couple of good points. Maybe it was me, was I going off on a tangent. If it was a murder, there has to be a motive. Right now the only thing that comes close to being a motive, is the chart. And I only have half of that puzzle solved.*

The sun had set and it was getting dark. I decided to try Mickey one more time before calling it a day. Mickey's lot was full, I was lucky to find a parking space on the street..

CHAPTER 10

I figured my timing was pretty good, I arrived at Mickey's between happy hour and the night crowd. The after work office throng was thinning out and the party animals hadn't arrived . Still his place was packed. I didn't see any empty stools at the bar but I did see Mickey hustling behind it. I wedged myself in at one end of the bar, between the wall and some macho type putting his moves on the red head to his left. I stood there for a couple of minutes listening to this guy's line, before I finally got Mickey's attention.

"What'll it be?" He didn't recognize me.

"Draft," He turned, reached for a glass under the bar and filled it at one of the taps.

"Remember me?" I said as he put the glass down in front of me.

He looked up and stared for a couple of seconds, then smiled. "Sure. Friend of Sean's, right?" You're, ah, Noah, right?"

"Right on both counts."

"Yeah, how you been?" He asked while wiping the bar.

"Good, say can we talk. I mean is there somewhere we can talk?"

"Sure, after closing. If you want to stick around till 3:30AM." He didn't wait for my reply, just moved off to take care of another customer. My timing wasn't so hot after all. The macho guy and the red head left together. I guess she bought his line. I moved to one of the vacated bar stools and stuck around for a couple more beers. Mickey was working the other end of the bar, and things began to look a little futile. I paid up and left. It was a warm night. The parking lot was now half empty as I crossed it, except for the two guys walking toward me.

As I went to pass, the one on the left grabbed my arm and spun me around, "Hey, what's the problem?" I barely got that out when the other guy sucker punched me in the kidneys. I went down hard on my knees. I put a hand to my back and tried to get up. The guy in front of me drop kicked my stomach. I went down flat on my face, scrapping my forehead, nose and right cheek. The other guy not to be out done, smiled and kicked me in the ribs. He must have been wearing a steel toed shoe. The pain was sharp, like being hit with an iron bar.

The blackness closed in masking the pain. As if in an echo chamber I heard a fuzzy voice say, "back off fucker, or next time you won't be walking." Then there was another kick to the ribs and I went out.

I don't know how long I laid there, but someone was shaking my shoulder. "Man you okay? Can you get up? Want me to call somebody?"

I couldn't get focused. I reached up with one of my hands and grabbed at an arm. My benefactor was a young black guy, wearing a Cleveland Indians baseball cap. "I guess I'll make it." I held my side with one hand and pulled on his arm with the other.

"Man you sure you gonna make it?" He helped me to my feet. My legs were a little rubbery. I held on to him to steady myself.

"I think so. Let me see if I can walk." I took a couple of steps, a little wobbly but I managed to support myself. "Hey thanks a lot man, I think I can make it." I let go of his arm.

"You sure? You don't look that great. What the hell happened anyway?" He held out his hand just in case I needed some support.

"Fell down. I'll be okay, my cars right on the street." I started to walk towards it. I was getting more steady with every step. "Thanks again." I gave him a little wave as I made my way to the street. Driving may be a problem, my ribs hurt like hell. I turned the corner of the building and headed up the street to West 9th.

Pulling on the lobby door sent a shooting pain all through me, I made my way to the intercom phone and punched in Monica's number.

"Yes." The familiar voice came over the phone.

"Monica it's me. Can you open up?"

"Noah? Is that you?"

"Yes. Open up."

"You sound funny."

"Monica please, press the buzzer." My head was getting a little fuzzy and I thought I was going to black out again. Finally she pressed the buzzer. I shuffled over to the elevator and rode it to the third floor, she was waiting for me as the elevator doors opened.

"Oh my God." She put her hands to her mouth. "What happened to you. I'm taking you to the hospital." She reached out to steady me.

"No. Please, let's just go inside." I limped toward her doorway.

"You look awful." I put one arm around her shoulder and she supported me as we walked. Once through the doorway, she let me down gently on to her couch. "Noah what happened? Were you in an accident? You really should see a doctor."

"Apparently I got in the way of two guy's who took there frustration out on me." She helped me off with my shirt. The skin in the area of my ribs was already turning a shade of deep purple. "Do you have any gauze? And some tape?" I asked.

"Yes, I will get it." She was back with some wet towels a roll of gauze and some tape. I winched at her touch, as she gently sponged me down. Then she wrapped the gauze tightly around my ribs, as I had directed. I remembered how to do this from my football days. Then she taped it tightly over the gauze. It felt a little better. Next she went into the kitchen and made some hot tea. I let myself ease into a prone position and closed my eyes. I fell asleep before the tea arrived.

I don't know how long I slept, but when I opened my eyes it was daylight. Monica was sitting on the floor next to the couch, holding my hand. She opened her eyes and let go of my hand when she felt me move.

"How do you feel?" She asked, turning toward me.

"Terrible. And hungry."

"Just stay there and I will make some coffee and breakfast." She scrambled to her feet and went into the kitchen. I did as I was instructed and waited for the next command. After a few minutes she came back into the room with a hot cup of coffee and set it down on the table next to me.

"Can you get up?"

"I think so." I shifted my weight and let my legs hang over the edge of the couch. It hurt like hell but with her help I managed to get into a sitting position, without letting out a scream. The coffee tasted great.

"I will make the eggs. Do you want to eat here or can you come to the kitchen?"

"Let me try to get up." I pushed down hard on the arm of the couch and got myself into a standing position. "I think I can make it. Let's eat in the kitchen."

We finished breakfast without my having to answer any questions, and sat at the table working on our second cup of coffee.

"Are you going to tell me what happened?" She had been patient and deserved some explanation.

"Sure." I went through the events of yesterday, my meeting with Mark, the trip to the library, my visit with Hank, my last stop at Mickey's and what took place afterward.

"Who were those men?" She asked.

"I don't have a clue. Maybe they were pissed at something and decided to take it out on me."

"But you said they gave you some kind of warning."

"Maybe they got the wrong guy." I shifted a little in my chair trying to get into a more comfortable position.

"Do you think this has anything to do with Sean?' She asked. Her face had the expression of deep concern.

"If it does, than I'm missing something. If I'm right about the chart, than I know where a lake freighter sunk. A freighter without a cargo, and one with no historical value. I don't think that would rate a beating and a warning." I finished my coffee.

"Maybe there is something you have overlooked in your research." She offered.

"Maybe? I made copies of everything at the library, it's all in my portfolio. Shit! All that stuff is in my car. Which I left parked on the street. The cop's probably had that thing towed by now."

"It is 7:30AM, Saturday morning. I do not think the police will bother with your car." She was confident.

"You're right. I forgot it's Saturday. Whoa, Saturday, I'm supposed to meet with the Kurtz's this morning." I started to get up, my ribs were killing me. "This is not going to be fun, I've got to get home and change."

"Noah, you are not going anywhere, except to lay back down. And that is an order. I will go to meet with the Kurtz's. Your father will be there to answer any construction questions and I can handle the rest. All I will need is your notes." There was no debating the situation. She was right. Monica could handle the Kurtz thing easily. She knew my ideas on the loft, I could not see any problem and if they had to talk to me they could always call.

"Are you sure you want to do this?

"I was going to meet you there anyway, so what is the problem" I guess there wasn't any.

"Not a thing. I guess a little more convalescence wouldn't hurt." I sat back down.

"I will go check on your car now and move it to my apartment lot." She was putting on her sneakers.

"Good idea. And while you are at it, bring up my portfolio and the cardboard box in the back seat." I decided to move to the couch for the rest of the day. But first I needed a shower no matter how much it hurt.

Monica brought up the stuff from my car and set it down next to the couch. She also re-taped me after my shower, and got me a terrycloth robe. Then she got herself ready for the Kurtz meeting. Before she left she put the phone close to me.

"After the meeting, I will run a few errands. I will call you before I come back in case you need anything." Then she bent down and gave me a much needed kiss.

I opened the box Mark Richter had given me. It was the stuff from Sean's desk at work. *"Not much here"*, some road maps a couple of street guides, one for Cleveland and one for Buffalo. Then the interesting stuff, a book entitled: "Learn Scuba Diving in One Weekend", another book: "The Divers Bible", and a receipt from the Erie Dive Shop, located in Westlake, a western suburb of Cleveland. I got out my note pad and wrote down the address. *"Looks like Sean was planning to or already did some diving, and I bet I know where."*

I put the stuff back into the box, but held on to the receipt. I grabbed my portfolio and dug out the micro film copies of the library information. I planned on spending the rest of the day re-reading the newspaper articles. I had this thought, *"It was interesting about the two names in Charles Campbell's address book."* Cliff Ingram and Smitty. One of the articles ran a list of the crew from the Alice Good, among the missing was a Cliff Ingram and a Calvin Smith. I pulled out the old High School yearbook I took from Mora's attic, and there they were, Campbell, Ingram and Smith, "Smitty" was his nick name. *"So the three of them went to high school together and were probably buddies."*

I continued to read the newspaper articles. *"Two million in gold bullion and a lake freighter disappear on the same day, without a* trace. And to this day, over 60 years later and nobody has found anything. Na-da, nothing, not a shred." "Coincidence? Maybe. And then Maybe not. What if the two events were tied together."

My mind was racing, *"Am I getting ahead of myself?" "What if the three of them, Campbell, Ingram and Smith were somehow responsible? Suppose they were the one's who robbed the train and somehow put the gold aboard the Alice Good and the ship sinks in a storm." "But before it sinks, the grid coordinates are recorded on a chart, and somehow Campbell comes into possession of that chart, he knows where the ship is and where the gold is, but then he's killed in the war. And now nobody knows." "Sixty-five years later Sean stumbles on the chart, figures out what it is, tells somebody about it and is killed for the chart." "It's a scenario and a motive."*

I picked up the morning paper and turned to the business section. *"Let's see gold is selling for nine hundred fifty an ounce at close of business on Friday. In 1941 the FBI calculated that the stolen gold bullion would have weighed about 1600 pounds, at nine hundred fifty an ounce, that's over twenty-four million in today's dollars. Now that's a motive!"*

"And I'll just bet my friend capt'n crunch is in it up to his eye balls. Sean showed him the chart, consulted him, he was the expert and he probably told Sean the markings were coordinates. Then Sean figured out the AG part and the rest of it. Then he told Mickey. Mickey had a boat they could be partners." "Ole' Mick must have loved that. Sean the poor schmuck." "The goons who worked me over were no doubt acting on behalf of capt'n crunch. He probably thinks I'm on to something or close to it. Now I had a real axe to grind. Now this was personal."

Monica got back around 1:00PM, carrying a couple of brown shopping bags. "How did it go?" I asked.

"Fine", she set the bags down, "Leonard was very pleased with the progress so far, he loves the idea of a juke box. And we still need two more chairs."

I knew Leonard Kurtz would go for the juke box idea. "Did he ask about me?"

"Yes. I told him and your father, that you were not feeling well. But that if need be, they could call you. Now how are you doing?"

Actually, all things considered I wasn't feeling too bad. I filled her in on my latest theory, such as it was. Lame as it might have been, it was all I had.

"Do you really think the gold is on that ship?" She asked.

"Yes, I think there is a good chance that it may very well be. Everything points in that direction, it's the only thing I can think of that would make that chart valuable.

"Noah you should go to the police." I reminded her that it was only a theory. What I needed was proof .

"What you need is your head examined." She looked frightened.

"Look what do you think the cop's will do, run over and arrest Mickey on my say so. Hardly. They believe it was a botched burglary, so they'd probably tell me to stop playing detective and keep my nose out of it."

"Maybe that is what you should do. If your theory is correct, this could be very dangerous. You may not be so lucky next time." She was real adamant.

"I'll tell you what. I've got this friend at the Cleveland Police Department, David Kaminski, I'll call him on Monday and run my theory by him. See what he say's." It was enough to make her smile. "In the meantime it's more rest and recuperation. But first I should get home and get some clean clothes."

"Never mind," she brought over one of the brown shopping bags. "I stopped at your place and picked up a few things." She pulled out a clean shirt, a pair of Dockers, underwear and socks. "And I stopped at Blockbuster and picked out three movies. We do not have to go anywhere for the next two days."

CHAPTER 11

The weekend rest was just what I needed, Monica did a great job nursing me back to almost a full recovery. My ribs still hurt and they were still taped, but I could drive in reasonable comfort and I could maneuver without wincing. The scratches on my face weren't too bad, shaving required a little more time and skill. In a couple more days the scratches should be just about gone. I called the Cleveland Police Homicide Division and asked for Lt. David Kaminski. A female voice answered the phone said he was very busy and could someone else help me. I told her no, and that it was very important that I talk to Kaminski. She took my name and put me on hold for a long time. Probably hoping I would hang up.

"Noah Wharton, as I live and breathe, to what do I owe a call from my favorite millionaire, and by the way the only millionaire I know personally." David would never let me forget that I won the Ohio Lottery.

"I'm glad you got that out of your system, now can we talk?"

"My aren't we touchy this morning."

"Look, be nice. I called to invite you to lunch."

"Lunch! That must mean you really need something pretty bad." I had not talked to David for some time, so I guess I had it coming. It did look rather obvious.

"Actually I need an impartial ear and some advice, are you available?"

"Well since you put it that way, how can I refuse. Besides I love it when you buy and I get to pick the spot."

"Who said anything about you picking the spot?"

"You mean after all this time, and the prospect of me doing you a favor, you would force me to eat at the Stadium Diner?"

"Okay, okay you win. Any other time I'd just keep this going, but I do need to talk to you. How about 11:30. You pick the spot."

"If you insist. I'll met you at Lucava's on East 9th. But it will have to be 1:00PM."

David Kaminski and I were classmates at Lakewood High

school, in our senior year David was all-city tight end and made the Cleveland Plain Dealer all state dream team the same year. I was a second string half back, I didn't get to play much, but I was on the team and that's all that mattered with the girls. David got a scholarship to Kent State University and graduated with a degree in criminology. He always wanted to be a cop. He married Kathy Gordon the homecoming queen, they have a couple of kids and live in Parma, a southwestern suburb of Cleveland. David planned his career path carefully and was well on his way up the ladder. He had been in the Homicide Division a little over a year and received two citations. I believe one day he will become chief.

After spending the morning reading about scuba diving from Sean's books, I was ready for a good lunch. Traffic was unusually heavy for this time of day and I arrived a little after 1:00, David was already seated.

"Noah, good to see you." He got up to shake my hand. At six foot two he had me by a couple of inches. David took care of himself. He weighed about 200 pounds, no flab, all muscle. Close cropped light brown hair, a light weight navy blue suit, white shirt and conservative tie. He looked more like an attorney, than a cop.

"Aw'right Kaminski, can we cut the crap and have a nice lunch." We shook hands, David loved to put people on, and if you didn't cut him off, he would just keep doing it.

"Right," he sat back down, "a nice lunch and some provocative conversation, isn't that what you said?"

I ignored the remark, "did you order yet?"

"No , actually, I just got here myself. And for the record, it is good to see you."

It was a good sign. He was being civil. "Thanks, it's good to see you." I picked up the menu. "What's good I'm really hungry."

We both ordered the 'blackened chicken', an antipasto and the house wine.

"So what have you been up to?" He asked. "Last I heard you were in Zurich."

"I was, but that was eighteen months ago. Boy we have been out of touch." I took a sip of the wine, "How about you? How are Kathy and the kids?"

"Everybody's fine. Kids are growing very fast. Michael is going to be ten next month. What about you. Anything serious going on in your life?"

"It all depends on what you call serious. I am involved with someone. We have discussed marriage. Right now Monica and I have an understanding and it's working out pretty well thanks."

He leaned back and was studying me. "You look like you have a problem Noah? What's on your mind?"

"I guess it is a problem, it's what I want to talk to you about. I need some impartial advice." Our lunch arrived and I decided to wait till we were finished before I continued.

I sipped my coffee and savored the lunch, "do you eat here often?" I asked.

"Not as often as I'd like too, can't afford it. Kathy and I come here on special occasion's and I come here without her when my millionaire friends are buying." He picked up his coffee cup and smiled.

"It was an excellent lunch." I said.

"So, are you going to tell me what's on your mind?" He asked.

"Yes I am." I told Dave everything from the beginning. Sean's death, Mora's suspicions, the missing chart, Mickey Kilbane, the mugging and my theory. He sat there attentively, silently, occasionally sipping his coffee and weighing my words. When I finished, we sat there for a couple of minutes before he spoke.

"I wondered about the scratches on your face, but frankly Noah, what you told me is pretty thin. It's a good theory, but you need more hard facts, more proof. The Lakewood police will just blow you off. Probably give you a warning for interfering in an open investigation, even though we both know they're probably not doing anything." The waiter refilled our coffee cups. "My advice to you, would be to cool it. Look, I'll call a guy I know over there and see what, if anything, they're doing. I'll run some of what you told me by him, without getting specific and see how it flies. I'll call you and let you know how it goes. Okay?"

"Okay."

"In the meantime you cool it. I'll also do some checking on Mickey, so you let that ride for now."

"Fine."

"I gotta tell ya' though, I like your theory. To bad this isn't a Cleveland case."

"I imagine if it was, you'd be right in it"

"Not right now. I'm TDY to another division."

"Oh yeah. What's that?" I asked.

"Would you believe the Burglary Unit. It all started with this stiff we fished out of the river. One thing led to another and I find myself evolved in a big deal case. Working with the Fed's no less, also Interpol and the RCMP from Canada. Some real heavy stuff."

"Really! What's it all about?"

"We figure the stuff is coming through Canada, into the Niagara/Buffalo area and then into Cleveland, where it's disposed of."

"Are you talking about drugs?" I asked, as I wasn't following his narrative.

"No, no, it's stones, gems; diamonds, rubies, you name it. We are talking hundreds of thousands of dollars." He finished his coffee.

"Sounds like you have your hands full. I'm sorry I bothered you with this."

"No problem, believe me it's no problem. And if I can help, you know I will." David Kaminski never let his friends down, he is a straight shooter and a very good cop.

After lunch I called Mora and set up a meeting for tonight. "Six o'clock will be fine, and I'll bring Monica and a pizza." Then I called Monica at work and told her about the meeting with Mora. "I'll pick you up at 5:00, on the Rockwell Avenue side."

"Did you have your meeting with your friend David Kaminski?" She asked with a tinge of skepticism in her voice. Like maybe I backed out on my promise.

"Yes I did. I'll tell you all about it when I see you."

"Good. I will see you at five." She seemed relieved.

It was only 3:00 when I finished talking to Monica, enough time for me to head on over to the Kurtz loft and check on the progress of the job. And to answer all the questions with regard to the state of my health I knew would be coming from my dad. My dad is a retired carpenter. He plied his trade for thirty-five years. When I bought the fire station he was responsible for doing the remodeling. He did a super job. So when I started getting clients and outside jobs, dad and I sort of formed a partnership. He operates as my general contractor, rounds up his old cronies from the trades, retired electricians, plumbers, masons, dry wall guys and the like. It saves me and my clients a lot of money, and they do a first rate job. Maybe a little slow, but first rate.

The loft was coming along nicely, I made a list of some things dad needed and promised to have them to him in the morning.

It was a little after five when I arrived at the Rockwell Avenue entrance to the Federal Reserve Bank, Monica was outside waiting.

"I just came from the loft," I said, as she slid into the front seat, "looks like the ceiling grid is working out."

"It does look nice," she said, "I like the way it cuts down on the ceiling height without giving up the sense of space."

"I like the light gray color of the grid against the black ceiling. Track lighting should work well with that set up." I added.

"I think it will be perfect." She said.

We drove over to my favorite pizza place on Detroit and as we sat waiting for our order I filled her in on my meeting with Dave Kaminski.

"Then you will take his advise?"

"That's what I told him. No waves till I hear from him." She had a skeptical look, "I promise."

"What are you going to tell Mora?" She asked.

"Everything I've found out so far. She's entitled to know that much, but I don't want to get her all worked up either." The pizza had arrived, I paid and we left for Mora's house.

"You're right on time, come on in." Mora led us to the kitchen.

We sat around the table eating pizza and drinking beer, not saying very much. Mora never mentioned the scratches on my face. Not that she should have. "I thought this would be a good time to bring you up to date." I set my beer down and wiped my mouth. "I have a theory, but it's just that, a theory." I proceeded to tell her about the chart and what I thought it meant. I also told her about my suspicion of Mickey Kilbane and my meeting with David Kaminski. I left out the little incident with the goons. Mora sat attentively through the whole narrative.

111

"So, where do we go from here?" She asked.

"We Wait. I want to see what Kaminski comes up with. Then we can plan our next move." I said. She nodded her head affirmatively.

"By the way," she said, "I got an odd piece of mail today." Mora got up to retrieve an envelope.

"Odd? How so?" I asked.

"It's a notice addressed to Sean, from a dive shop. It say's his scuba gear is in." She had a puzzled look on her face.

"Really, let me see." I reached out and took the envelope from her. "Interesting, this kind of confirms part of my theory."

"I don't understand?" She said.

"Sean probably came to the same conclusion I did, about the ship Alice Good. He was planning to check it out." I explained.

"But Sean never did any diving. Why didn't he confide in me, why didn't he say anything?" I could see she was a little upset by the thought that there might have been secrets between them.

"Mora, do not blame yourself." Monica injected. "I am sure Sean was not keeping secrets. He never had the chance to tell you." Monica put her hand on Mora's to reassure her.

"That's right. I don't think it means anything. I don't think he was holding back, he just never had the chance."

"I suppose you're right." She snapped out of it. "Would you like another beer?"

"Sure," I was quick to answer.

"None for me," said Monica. "I still have half a bottle."

"Mora do you mind if I keep this notice?" I asked.

"No. Not at all." She replied.

I took a sip of the fresh bottle of beer she set before me, "can you think of anyone outside of us and Hank, Denise and Mickey Kilbane, that Sean might have mentioned the chart to?"

"He probably told others, but I don't know who specifically. He had the chart for a few weeks. I'm sure he did some research as you did, but I don't know who in particular he would have talked to. Maybe someone at this dive shop." She pointed to the piece of mail.

"Maybe." We left Mora's around 9:00PM.

"She did not comment on the gold?" Monica recalled as we drove back to my place.

"I think she's still in a daze. Besides it's a theory. We have nothing concrete. I need to get proof." I turned the Cherokee onto West 117th.

"What do you mean proof? I thought you said you were not going to do anything till you heard from your friend David."

"I'm not. I just thought maybe I'd check on this dive shop. I'm not going anywhere near Mickey's, so how much trouble can I get into?" I pulled up behind the fire station. She gave me a look, like *'here we go again'*. "Monica," I continued, "How would you like to take scuba lessons?"

"I knew it." She was trying to look upset, but I knew she was interested. When it comes to investigating and mysteries, Monica is as bad as I am. She has a curiosity streak. She smells adventure and she's hooked.

"Look I'll go over and check out this dive shop, see what it's all about. If it looks good, I'll sign us up. It'll be fun." She sat there smiling. Not saying a word. "Besides, I've got to prove my theory. Without a motive there is no way anyone is going to take me seriously. Finding that ship and the gold would make one hell of a motive."

"Yes it would." She turned to me, "let's do it!"

CHAPTER 12

The Lake Erie Dive Shop was located out in Westlake on Dover Center Road. The dive shop was located in a strip plaza, with ten other stores. I got there around 9:30AM, I figured the shop probably opened at 9:00. I was wrong. It opened at 10:00AM. The sign on the door read: Jerry Malone, Proprietor. Fortunately there was a donut shop two doors down from the dive shop. I ordered coffee and a donut and waited for the dive shop to open.

I left the donut shop exactly at 10:00, as I turned heading toward the dive shop a young man, about six foot tall, long blond hair, lean and well tanned, wearing a T-shirt and faded jeans was inserting a key into the door lock. I guessed it was Jerry Malone. I followed him inside.

"Good morning." He said with a pleasant smile.

"Good morning," I repeated, "you must be Jerry Malone."

"Yes, that's right. How did you know?" He opened the cash register drawer and put the door key in the tray.

"I could tell you I was psychic, but actually it was the sign on the door."

"Oh yeah." Even a bigger smile. "How can I help you?"

"Mr. Malone." I put my hands on the counter.

"Please, call me Jerry." He interrupted.

"Jerry it is," I took the notice out of my pocket. "You sent this notice to a friend of mine." I showed him the notice, "I'd like to pick up whatever it was that he ordered."

"He didn't tell you what it was?" Jerry asked.

"Well no. You see he couldn't." I explained the situation .

"Gee I'm sorry." He was very understanding. It took a few minutes for him to retrieve the package from the back room. He set the large box on the counter.
"What is it?" I asked.

"A wet suit, mask, gloves, fins, boots, BC vest, console and flashlight. A complete set of diving gear. The best!" He went through the box for my benefit, to make sure everything was there.

"Looks like he was all set to do some serious diving." I said.

"He was taking lesson's for a few weeks, and was pretty much set to strike out on his own. As soon as this stuff arrived. It's been here for a couple of weeks. That's why I sent the notice."

"How much do I owe you?" I asked.

"It's all paid for." He said, putting everything back in the box.

"Do you think that stuff would fit me?"

"Probably. We could find out for sure. I've got a dressing room over in the corner. You could try on the suit." He took it out of the box and held it out to me.

"Why not," I said. I took the suit from him. He gave me some instructions on how to put it on and I headed for the dressing room.

He studied me as I came out of the dressing room, "is it comfortable? Not too confining?" He asked.

"Seems okay." I felt like a cast member of Sea Quest.

"It looks okay." He walked around me tugging at the suit. "I'd say it fits." Giving it his final approval.

"Good," I said. "Now how about a suit for a female. Have you got one in stock?"

"How tall and what does she weigh?"

116

"Five six, about a hundred and ten."

"Yeah, I think we can manage one. She would have to come in and try it on."

"No problem. How about the rest of this stuff? Got duplicates?" I asked.

"Sure. The vest and the rest of the gear is no problem. If I haven't got it in stock, only takes a couple of days to get it. So we're golden."

"Great! How late are you open?"

"Till 7:00 tonight."

"How about lesson's. Do you give scuba instructions?"

"Sure do. Wednesday and Friday, afternoons and evenings and all day Saturday and Sunday."

"Great. I'd like to sign up two for the weekend, Friday, Saturday and Sunday." I gave him the necessary information. He told me I would need to get a fitness physical and gave me the necessary forms and a list of doctors. I told him I would be back around 6:00 with Monica for her fitting. I paid for Monica's stuff and the lessons, then left.

Jerry Malone told me as long as both of us were decent swimmers we should be able to go it alone after a weekend of intense instruction. That would be twelve lessons, twelve hours. We could rent what we did not buy. It sounded good. When I called Monica with the news, she couldn't wait to get started. She

117

wanted to know what color my suit was and did she have a choice of colors?

"Of course." I said, "we could have matching suits." She didn't think black and yellow was such a great combination.

We decided that after our weekend of lessons, we could practice all week till the following weekend, then we could go looking for the Alice Good. It sounded like a reasonable plan.

We made appointments to get our physicals on Wednesday. We both checked out 100%, except the doctor did take notice of my rib bruises and cautioned against my taking any deep dives for a couple of weeks. I did not mention this to Monica. My wet suit would cover the bruises so no attention would be drawn to my problem. Nobody would ask questions, like the instructor for one.

Hank called on Thursday to check on a weekend car show in Akron, Ohio and to coordinate our plans for the July Fourth Classic Car gathering. It was being held this year, on the spacious grounds of the Wavecrest Hotel, adjacent to Pine Point Amusement Park on Sandusky Bay.

In the world of classic cars, the July Fourth Classic is a big deal event. The Great Lakes Region of the Classic Car Owners Club of America, to which Hank and I both belong, is the host for this event. C.C.O.C.A. is a national organization with chapters and regions all over the U.S. including Hawaii, Alaska and all of Canada. Every year there are two types of shows conducted by the various regions. A local event and a national event. In order to gain stature and subsequently increase the value of your car, you must compete and win in these events.

The first prestigious award is called a Junior First, the other a coveted Senior First. The only way to win either or both is to win at a sanctioned National Meet. The first time your car wins, that's called a Junior First. At the next national meet your car must win a first place again and that's called a Senior First You must win first at two successive meets. Judging at these events is fierce. If I attend a national meet it's usually without my vintage car, or with my car in the Not To Be Judged category. I'm just not cut out for this high end competition. It's not my bag. I love old cars, but I love them for other reasons then competing for a trophy. The local meets, that's different. It's fun to compete in those. It's not as serious. Hank on the other hand goes out for blood. He has two Junior Firsts and one Senior First.

The Great Lakes Region is very active in C.C.O.C.A. and therefore carries a lot of weight. With that said, the July Fourth meet becomes a big deal event, because it's sanctioned as a national meet. And I know nothing is going to stop Hank from showing his new toy, the Mark V Coupe.

The July Fourth meet is great, it's not just the show itself, there is a whole weekend of extra curricular side trips, planned and unplanned cocktail parties, and the fun of being within the amusement park. It's going to be a three day event, beginning on Friday and ending with an awards banquet on Sunday. Hank and I booked our rooms at the Wavecrest six months ago. I could tell from his conversation that he was salivating. He was going to test the waters this weekend at the Siberling Hall meet in Akron, Ohio. It's a nice local event, draws about 250 cars from a number of clubs in the area.

"Sorry Hank, we made other plans."

"But I'm taking the Mark V, I thought you'd enjoy seeing me cream the competition. A warm up to the National. Sure you won't change your mind?"

"No can do."

"But what's so important that would keep you from the Siberling thing?" He was pressing, he knew I liked the show.

"Monica and I have committed ourselves to some scuba lessons. And I've already paid for them. Hey, I'm really sorry, I completely forgot about Siberling, and she's all keyed up for scuba." I pleaded my case.

"Scuba! What's with scuba diving? You planning a trip somewhere, like the Caymans maybe?"

"No. Just something we have always wanted to do." I lied, not wanting to tell him the real reason.

"I see, well I guess you have to do what you have to do, but we'll miss you guys. He was not happy. "By the way how's it going with your Sean investigation? You still on that? Anything new?"

"No, not really, still pretty much a dead end."

"Well keep me posted, if there's anything I can do, you know where to find me. Call ya' on Monday."

"Yeah, let me know how you make out at the show." There was a click and he hung up, I'm not sure he heard me. He still thought that I was wasting my time. Chasing ghosts just to appease Mora. I was not ready to accept the facts that Sean's death was accidental. There was a time when I probably would have agreed, but not anymore. Especially not after my encounter with the two goon's in Mickey's parking lot, and what I knew about the 'Alice Good'.

I was working at the loft on Friday when Dave Kaminski called. He called at 10:00 AM and left a message on my machine. He found nothing unusual on Mickey Kilbane and pronounced him 'clean'. I still didn't buy it. He had to be involved. I picked up the phone and called my friend Max Thursday.

Max and I go back to my days at Great Western Casualty, before I won the lottery and quit my job. Max is a Private Investigator. He did work for me from time to time on some insurance cases. Max is sixty-something, he lives on a two acre spread in North Royalton, which is a suburb south of Cleveland. During those Great Western days we became good friends. He taught me how to fly and helped me get a P.I. license. He became my mentor, and was a little disappointed that I did not pursue a career as a Private Investigator. He said I had the gift of a natural snoop, but he understood.

CHAPTER 13

Maxwell Nathan Thursday, Lieutenant Colonel, U.S. Air Force, retired. He was a fighter pilot during the Korean War, and was credited with four kills, when he was shot down by a Chinese MIG, while flying a ground support mission. It left him with a badly damaged lung . No longer fit to fly jets, Max flew as a FAC (Forward Air Controller) pilot in Vietnam. After two tours he was finally grounded and assigned to a desk.

The last five years of his active service he spent in a C.I.D. (Criminal Investigation Division) unit of the Air Police. When he finally retired, with 25 plus years, he became a Private Investigator, putting the CID skills to work. Max is likable, somewhat laid back in his demeanor, but at the same time he is tenacious and shrewd. I like Max for a number of reasons, not the least of which being, that he has an appreciation for old cars. His tastes in old cars are a little different from mine, he likes Chrysler product cars of the 1940's. He is not a collector as such, but he does own a pristine 1948 Chrysler Town and Country convertible. He doesn't show it, he drives it. But only in the summer, and only on sunny days, when he can put the top down. He say's at his age old cars are to drive, not show.

Max is a man of few words and many talents. Among his resources he has a two place, single engine, Kit Fox. A retractable wing aircraft that he built himself. He keeps it along with a gyro-copter and the Town and Country in a hanger type building on his North Royalton property. The three acre property also includes a 1,000 ft grass air strip. He also owns a 27ft Wellcraft, cabin cruiser, with a 140 horse power Volvo engine. Which he docks in Vermillion, Ohio. A small port town on Lake Erie, about 40 miles west of Cleveland.

I have not seen or talked to Max for some time, but he never seems to get upset at my not keeping in touch. I think about him from time to time, and this was one of those times.

"Hello."

"Hi Max, it's Noah."

"Hi kid, how's it going?" Same old Max, it's as if we just talked a couple of days ago.

"Fine Max, how have you been?"

"I'm do'in okay, so what's on your mind?" Max is not one for idle conversation, gets right to the point.

"I may have a job for you, if you're interested. Can we meet for lunch?"

"Yeah, sure. Where and when?"

"How about 12:30 today at Fast Freddies on Pearl Road."

"Sounds good to me. See you at 12:30, I'll be the guy with the white hair." Click, he hung up. Good old Max, it was good to hear his voice.

I advised my dad that I would be gone for a couple of hours and left the job site around 11:45. I pointed the Jeep Cherokee south and headed for Fast Freddies in Parma, a southwest suburb of Cleveland, next door to North Royalton. It was 12:20 when I arrived. I recognized the faded red Ford pick-up, the paint may have been dull, but there wasn't a rust spot on it. Max was already here. This was his surveillance vehicle. He sat in a booth facing the door, with his face stuck in a menu. He raised his head and waved me over.

"Good to see you Max." I put out my hand as he rose.

"Good to see you kid." We shook hands.

"Lets order ," he said, "then we'll talk."

I nodded my head in agreement and looked at the menu. Fast Freddies is a gourmet hamburger drive-in restaurant. They are noted for their cheeseburgers and deep fried onion rings. I ordered both.

"Okay let's have it. What's on your mind?" Max does not waste time.

"I'll fill you in from the beginning, so you'll have the whole picture." I told him the whole story. Sean's death, the chart, Alice Good, my theory about the gold, Mickey Kilbane, and the mugging. "So what do you think?"

"It looks like you pretty much got it worked out, where do I fit in?"

"Right now I figure Mickey Kilbane is my number one suspect. The cops have marked him clean, but I'm not convinced. I would like you to do some digging into Mr. Kilbane. That is if you don't have anything else going on right now. What do you say? Can you do it?" He thought it over all of thirty seconds, long enough for him to take a swallow of his coke.

"I've got nothing on the table right now so it's a go."

"Great!" I said.

"One question," he took another swallow of his coke, "Is this still an open homicide investigation?"

"The Lakewood cops are still carrying it as open, but they are convinced that it's a botched burglary, I don't think they're working very hard at proving it otherwise. I think it's still open because Mora keeps on them."

"Be that as it may, I just want to know where I stand. I don't like surprises, and I don't want any backlash."

"Fair enough. The usual fee alright?"

"Yeah that'll be fine. Now give me some data to work with." He took out a small spiral bound notebook and pen, clicked the point down.

I gave him dates in sequence of events, Mickey's address, location of his bar, where he keeps his boat, some of the Alice Good info, with the exception of the grid coordinates. Our lunch arrived and we ate in silence, enjoying the food. Max finished his burger, sat back, and drank some of his coke.

"You still got those German cars?" he asked.

"Yeah, as a matter of fact I do." I smiled.

"Are they still stashed in that Lakewood garage?" He put away the pen and notebook.

"No, I've got myself a new place."

"You mean the old fire station?"

"How did you know?" I asked, with the look of amazement on my face.

"I keep track of my friends." He smiled.

"You'll have to come out sometime and give the place the once over. I think you'll like what I've done with it."

"I will definitely do that." We both got up out of the booth. "Thanks for lunch. I'll be in touch."

"Thanks Max. I'll wait to hear from you." With Max on the case I felt a lot better. He knew how to dig and his info was always without question.

CHAPTER 14

As I left the restaurant a different scenario was playing out across town.

Chuck Preebe was in the process of detailing a superb 1948 Packard Custom Eight convertible. The black paint finish gleamed under the florescent lights of the shop. He had finished cleaning the smooth red leather interior and was now tackling the trunk. As Chuck removed the spare tire something rolled on to the trunk mat. It sparkled a deep red. The little stone was about the size of a raisin. He picked it up and rolled it around in his hand. "Pretty thing", he thought. The stone reminded him of the visit he had earlier this week from that Cleveland cop. "What the hell was his name?" Then he remembered the card he had been given. He reached into his coverall pocket and extracted the white card, it read: Lt. David Kaminski, City of Cleveland, Police Department. There was an address on Payne Avenue and a telephone number with an extension.

"I wonder if I should call this guy?" He flicked the card across his lips, while fondling the stone between his figures. "It sure looks real." He paused. "I guess I better." He walked over to the phone, picked it up and dialed Kaminski's number.

He was informed by the switchboard operator that Lt. Kaminski was out of the office and could someone else help him. He told the operator that he would rather talk to Kaminski. He left his name and number, with the assurance from the operator that his message would be relayed, and Kaminski would get back to him.

Chuck put the gem stone in his handkerchief, folded it and stuffed it into the pocket of his coveralls. He returned to his work There was still a lot to do. He would be working late to finish the job. The car was to be picked up in the morning.

Chuck had been detailing classic cars for twenty years and had gained a reputation for outstanding workmanship. The shop always had one or two classics on hand at all times, awaiting his skilled hands and keen eye. He began to vacuum the cavernous interior of the trunk and waited for Kaminski to return his call.

East of the city, in the suburb of Pepper Pike two men were engaged in a heated conversation.

"Look I counted the stones, there's one missing, what the fuck do you want from me? Maybe we were shorted on the other end. Did you ever consider that?" The man seated behind the desk was pleading his case. He was in his early forties, black wavy hair, with an olive complexion that reflected his Mediterranean ancestry. He was well dressed, a dark blue suit, bright white shirt with gold cuff links and he was wearing a gold Rolex. His hands were perfectly manicured, a large black onyx ring on the third finger of his right hand.

"Come off it Tony, you know damn well it wasn't shorted on the other end. Now cut the shit and lets find out where that missing stone is. When did you retrieve the bag?"

The tall younger man standing in front of the desk was broad shouldered, with a big chest, his hair was cut short. At sometime in the past he had been an athlete. He was casually dressed and working on a tan, right now he was a little more red than tan, and his hair was a little sun dried, like someone that spent a lot of time on the water. He had been doing most of the yelling and now lowered his voice and talked in a calm manner.

"I took it out of the car this morning before I dropped it off at Marshall's for detailing. I want to have it ready for the July Fourth Classic show."

"You asshole. Why the hell take that car to a show? You've got others. I don't fucking believe you." The younger man paced the floor shaking his head.

"Fuck you. It's a great car. What the hell is wrong with you?"

"Where did they plant it?"

"It was under the carpeting in the trunk, behind the spare. In this cloth bag." Replied Tony holding up the bag.

"Did you have any trouble getting it out?"

"No, not really. A few of the stones fell out of the bag, it wasn't tied very securely. Maybe three or four, but I'm sure I got them all."

"Yeah, right. Why the fuck didn't you tell me this in the first place?" His voice began to raise. "Shit. That's probably where it's at."

"What do you mean?" Tony was puzzled.

"It's probably still in the trunk." Then he mumbled under his breath, "dumb son-of-a-bitch."

"So what do we do now?" Asked Tony.

"Well I guess we go get it, what else. We'll go after the garage closes."

Kaminski picked up his messages at the switchboard. He thumbed through them as he walked down the hall to his office. He sat down at his desk and held out one of the pink slips. He looked at the name written on it and tried to put a face to it.

"Chuck Preebe, Chuck Preebe? Oh yeah, the little guy at Marshall's garage." There was no message just his name and phone number and the time the call came in 4:45, it was almost 6:00PM and it was Friday.

"Probably gone for the day." He said to himself. *"I'll call him first thing Monday."* He put the message on a spindle, and sorted though the rest of his calls. It looked like he was going to be here awhile. *"Better call the wife."*

Tony and his partner arrived at the garage a little before 9:00 PM, it was dusk. Expecting to find the garage dark and empty,

129

they were surprised to see lights through the windows.

"I guess we better have a look."

"Yeah. Right." Replied Tony.

They both approached one of the wire meshed windows cautiously and peered inside. They could see Chuck Preebe working on Tony's car. It appeared that he was alone. They moved away from the window and walked to the door at the side of the building. They banged on the door very hard. It took awhile before Chuck heard the banging. He shut off the buffer, laid it on the floor and walked over to the door. He was cautious, who would be here at this hour, he wondered.

"Who is it," he asked standing near the door.

"It's Mr. Valentine, Chuck. Came down to check on my car, you want to open up."

Chuck looked through the small square of a wire mesh window on the door to verify the voice. Satisfied, he unlatched the dead bolt and slid back the security bar, then opened the door and admitted the two men.

8:30 AM, it was his day off, David Kaminski was having a leisurely breakfast, when the call came. It was the Precinct Captain, "sorry to bother you on your day off, but there was a homicide at 3605 Carnegie Avenue. The victim had one of your cards, I thought you may be interested in checking it out first hand." It wasn't an order, but Kaminski thought he better have a look. Horwitz was the detective in charge on the scene, Kaminski's old partner.

Kaminski drove to the Carnegie address, which didn't register with him until he got there. It was Marshall's Garage. Uniformed police had already taped off the area. He found Howitz in the garage talking to one of the employee's.

"What's up Sam?" Kaminski asked, as he pulled on a pair of latex gloves.

"Hello Dave, I believe you are acquainted with the victim. One Charles Preebe." Horwitz motioned to the body lying on the garage floor covered with a blanket.

Kaminski walked over, knelt down and pulled back the blanket. It was Preebe alright. He was tied to a chair, hands tied behind his back. Someone or somebody beat the hell out of him, then put two bullets in his chest.

"What do you make of it?" Kaminski asked, looking up at Horwitz.

"We got the call around 7:40 AM. The shop manager opened up and found the body. Black and White was first on the scene and secured the area. Looks like the perp gained entrance through the side door. No forcible entry, so the victim probably knew his assailant. Sterling is outside looking around, I just started talking to the shop manager, guy named Wilkes. Want to sit in?"

"No you go ahead, I'll catch up with Sterling. By the way how did you put me together with Preebe?"

"Your card in his pocket. Anything you want to talk about?"

"Later. Did you call forensic?"

131

"Yeah, on the way."

Kaminski took another look at Preebe. Apparently the force of the shots knocked him and the chair over. A handkerchief was laying beside him, which struck Kaminski as odd. Not like someone wiped their hands and dropped it. It was folded and relatively clean. He replaced the blanket and went looking for Sterling. Kaminski noted as he exited the side door that there was a dead bolt and slide bar, both were undone.

Sterling was outside , examining the area around the rear of the building, "find anything", asked Kaminski, rounding the corner of the building.

"Not so far. Horwitz tell ya', we found your card on the vic."

"Yeah, he did."

"Nothing out here that I can see. Looks like the perp, or perps, entered through the side door. We did find a couple of 25 caliber casing around the body."

"Twenty-five huh, Professional hit?"

"Could be?" Replied Sterling.

"Yeah but a little messy don't you think?"

"Not very neat." Sterling agreed.

Kaminski headed back inside, with Sterling trailing behind. Horwitz headed over when he saw them.

"What did you get from the manager?" Asked Kaminski.

"He say's Preebe was working late on the Packard. That's the old black convertible. They promised to have it ready this morning. Manager say's that it looks like Preebe was almost finished with the job. So it couldn't have been too late."

"Looks like you boys got your work cut out, sorry I can't stick around and give you a hand." Said Kaminski

"You gonna tell me about the card?" Asked Horwitz.

"I talked to Preebe earlier this week, about some matter I'm working on, is all."

"The TDY shit." said Horwitz.

"Yeah."

"How much longer they got you tied up with that stuff?"

"Don't know. Till it gets done I guess. Listen, copy me on the report and the Coroners findings." As Kaminski left he made note of the Packard's license, it was one of those vanity plates. It read: PAKARD. When he got back to his office he ran the plate. He sat down at this desk and removed the pink message slip from the spindle. The one with Preebe's name on it. He wondered why Preebe was calling him. When he got the information on the plate, Kaminski picked up the phone and put in a call to Noah. The machine answered, so he left a message.

By 9:30 the Coroner had removed the body and the forensic team was working on the area under the body. They also examined the Packard and were dusting the side door of the building. They removed a single sheet of paper from the glove box, put it in an envelope and tagged it.

CHAPTER 15

Most Monday mornings are slow going, this particular Monday was even more so. The weekend of scuba lessons had taken it's toll. I was bushed and had to force myself out of bed and into the real world. It was 10:00 AM by the time I showered and was working on my second cup of coffee. There was one message on my machine from the weekend. It was Dave Kaminski. Maybe he had something on Mickey. I picked up the phone and returned his call.

"Kaminski." He answered on the first ring.

"Dave it's Noah."

"Noah, thanks for returning my call, listen do you still belong to that Classic Car Club?"

"Yes I do. Why?"

"I've been working on something and you may be able to help me out. Are you free anytime this afternoon?" He asked.

"Yeah sure. I mean I could make myself free. What's on your

mind?"

"How about meeting me at the little coffee chop around the corner from you, the Continental. Say 3:00, it should be quiet at that time of day. We'll be able to talk and I'll fill you in."

"Look, if you want a quiet place to talk, why not just come on over to my place."

"Okay by me." He hadn't protested, didn't even try. "See you at 3:00."

Curious, I thought. I wonder what that was all about. Whatever it was I'd have to wait till this afternoon. In the meantime there is work to be done. The rest of the morning I spent going over material invoices. The Kurtz loft project was nearing completion.

Around noon I went over to the job site and checked in with my dad. We discussed a few things, made some changes and I was back at the fire station by 1:00 PM. I decided it was a good time to give Mora a call.

"Hi Mora"

"Hi Noah."

"I'm glad I caught you at home, I'd like to bring you up to date. First off Monica and I decided to take scuba lesson's. It's something we've always wanted to do and proving out my theory gives us an excuse. We should be able to dive on the Alice Good in about a week." She listened without interrupting. "Second, I've asked a detective friend of mine to look into Mickey Kilbane. I'm betting the old map is the key and Mickey's involved."

135

"You really think Sean was killed for a treasure map?"

"Right now it's the only motive I have. If I'm right and there is a treasure, then it's one heck of a motive."

"But where does Mickey Kilbane fit in."

"Right now it's only a gut feeling. I haven't got any real proof, but I'm working on that. I guess we'll just have to wait and see."

"Whatever you think. But the scuba thing is a little scary. How does Monica feel about all of this?" She sounded a little leery.

"Monica agrees. Scuba is something we've always talked about doing and we have an excellent instructor. I don't see any real problems." I tired to reassure her.

"If we should find the ship and there is gold aboard, I'll turn the whole thing over to the police."

"You know best."

"Look there is one thing I need you to do. I want you to file a salvage claim on the 'Alice Good' with the state of Ohio."

"Okay. But how do I do that?"

"You'll need to go to the state office building. It's that black building on the corner of Superior and West 9th. Go to the information counter, they'll direct you. File the claim in your name. I'll give you a description of the vessel. You'll also need to identify the cargo. Just put down artifacts, quantity unknown."

"I'll do it tomorrow." she said.

"That'll be fine. If you have any problems call me. Otherwise I'll be in touch with you before the weekend."

CHAPTER 16

Kaminski was right on time. The buzzer at the street level door sounded precisely at 3:00. I pressed the lock release button. I heard Kaminski on the stairs and opened the apartment door as he reached the landing.

"Hi Dave. Wow, great place." He said, as he entered and casually surveyed the great room.

"Thanks. Let me show you around." I guided him around the apartment, giving him the grand tour. My office, the bedroom, exercise room and kitchen. Then we descended the circular staircase to the garage. I showed him my two cars. After spending half an hour discussing the cars and the garage itself, we headed back up the stairs.

"How about a cold beer?" I asked.

"Sure, I could use one."

I took a couple of cold Sam Adams out of the refrigerator and we settled into a pair of comfortable chairs.

"What's up?" I asked.

"Noah, the last time we met I told you I was on a temporary duty assignment with the burglary unit. I'd like to tell you a little about the case I've been working on. I think you may be able to help me. Are you game?"

"I'm not sure I follow you. But if I can help, then sure, I'm in."

"What I'm about to tell you is strictly confidential. My ass is on the line here."

"No problem, fire away." I said, in a controlled voice, although my curiosity was way up.

"Noah I don't want to put you in jeopardy, so after hearing me out, you want to pass, I'll understand and it's ok."

"Geez Dave you're not trying to scare me are you? Half kidding, but a little more than curious.

"Look I'll just get to the point. You be the judge."

The scenario Dave layed out went something like this: There was this theft ring operating in Europe. They were stealing jewelry, expensive jewelry, large stones, gold and silver settings. Interpol traced the stuff to Canada, where the stones were removed from their settings. The gold and silver were melted down into bullion. Small bars. The stones were then smuggled across the border into the U.S. via Buffalo and subsequently to Cleveland, where they were reset into new settings and sold as estate jewelry.

The Cleveland police, Interpol, the RCMP and the FBI were all involved as a joint task force. They had a good line on how the stuff got to Canada and were closing in on the smelting operation. They also had a line on a well known Cleveland estate jeweler who was remounting the stones. The missing piece was; how did the stones get from Canada to Cleveland.

"I've got a theory, " Dave said. "I think they are being smuggled across the border in antique cars."

"You're kidding! How do you figure that one?

"I don't think it started out that way." He continued. "Initially, I think they were brought in by boat, small craft, pleasure boats, and that's how we tracked down the local jeweler. We tightened that up, by having the Coast Guard step up random searching, at sea and on shore. It made the risk to great, so I think they figured out an alternative method."

"So you think antique car collectors are smuggling the stolen jewelry into the U.S."?

"No, not generally, but specifically. A small group of men, who happen to be car collectors and one thing in common."

"And what's that?" I asked.

"They all belong to the Classic Car Owners Club. Live in the Cleveland area, and have purchased Classic Cars out of Canada in the last eight months."

"Whoa. Are you serious? Is that why you called me?" This was troubling.

"My problem is I have no proof. " He leaned back in his chair and finished off his beer.

"So where do I fit in?"

"I've got it down to three suspects. All respectable. All collectors, all members of your club, and all have purchased two or more cars out of Canada in the last eight months."

"And you want me to do what?"

"I think I've found a way to tie in one of them. And with that, I'm hoping with enough pressure, he'll cooperate. Turn states evidence and implicate the others." He played with the empty beer bottle.

"You still haven't answered my question. How do I fit in?"

"Saturday morning a garage mechanic by the name of Preebe was found murdered in his garage. We haven't released any details to the press. I think this may be the break we've been looking for."

"Not Chuck Preebe?"

"One and the same. Did you know him?" asked Dave.

"Yes I did. He did some work on my Mercedes. Helluva nice guy. Who'd want to kill him?"

"Good question. He called me Friday afternoon and left a message. He wanted to tell me something, but we never made contact. Saturday he was found dead with two slugs in his chest."

Watching him play with the empty beer bottle . I finally got the hint. "Listen, you want another beer?"

"Yeah, sure." He handed me his empty. I retrieved a couple more cold ones and settled back down in my chair.

"The car Preebe was working on belonged to one of my suspects and was recently brought here from Canada." He held up his hand before I could say anything. "That may be a coincidence, but I don't think so. I think Preebe was calling me about that car. And whatever it was got him killed."

"You think the car owner killed him?"

"During the autopsy the Coroner was able to lift a thumb print from his wrist. We were lucky, a few hours later and he couldn't have done that. And here's the good part. In the glove box of the car we found a customs release form, and it had a perfect thumb print, which matched to one we got off Preebes' wrist. I figure the print belongs to the car owner. If it does, it would go a long way to confirm my theory. Incidentally the port of entry was Niagara Falls, New York."

"So you have your killer."

"Well, sort of."

"Sort of?"

"We ran both prints through our R.K.C. and came up with nothing. No known criminal or juvenile record in the state of Ohio, for either print. The FBI is checking their AFIS system, but that can take up to a week. Our department recently came on line with the FBI's "Latent Cognizant Data Base" and that came up with a big zero. So I've got two prints that match, and I believe they belong to the same guy, the guy that owns the car; but I can't prove it." Dave took a swig of his beer.

"Who's the guy?" I asked.

"Anthony Valentine."

"Tony!!" I blurted out, coughing, trying to swallow my beer. "No way!" I couldn't believe what I was hearing.

"This is where you come in. That is, if you're game."

"What!"

"Look, if you want to prove it's not him, fine. For whatever reason you do this, it's fine with me."

"Exactly what is it you want me to do?"

"I want you to get a right hand thumb print. Discreetly. If I could do this any other way I would. We can't just bring him in and fingerprint him. His attorney would have a field day. It would blow our whole investigation. We have no probable cause. I think you can help us, but I don't want to compromise you. So if you say no. It's ok.

"You sure there's no other way?"

"None that would be easier." He said.

"So when and how am I to do this."

"The sooner the better. When's your next meeting?"

"That's not until the end of next month." I said. Then I thought a minute. "We do have this car show coming up on the fourth.

The forth of July weekend."

"That's perfect. With all that will be going on I'm sure he'll never suspect."

"I don't know Dave. I mean I've known this guy for a few years. This is kind of shitty." I guess I was doing some back peddling, even before I actually made a firm commitment.

"Well that's really up to you, but just remember poor ole Preebe, didn't deserve those two slugs, didn't deserve to die." Dave was making a strong point.

"Certainly not. But how can you be so sure Tony is your man?"

"That's just it. I'm not. So maybe you'll be doing him a favor."

I thought about that. I guess if I was trying to prove his innocence this was as good a way as any. So I made the commitment.

He outlined a plan. If I could get his print on a glass or similar surface that would be ideal. I just had to watch for the opportunity. I would have a couple of day's to work on it. Tony was the clubs' V.P., so he would be around and actively involved. I'm sure we would cross paths during the course of the weekend, I'd just have to watch for my opportunity."

That done, Dave and I had another beer, and talked a little about Mickey Kilbane. I asked him about the message he left me, regarding Mickey being clean. He confirmed that Mickey had an alibi for the night Sean was killed. He worked the bar that day from 2:00 in the afternoon till closing. Apparently one of his afternoon people called in sick.

"How convenient." I thought. Dave asked if I was still investigating Mickey. I told him I was keeping my distance. That I decided to take up scuba diving.

"Scuba diving!" He gave me a quizzical look. "You're not thinking of looking for that sunken freighter?"

"Yes I am. I need to know that it's really there."

"How much do you know about diving?" He asked.

"I've been taking lessons for over a week."

"A week! Man you are nut's."

"I know it's sounds crazy, but I've got a super instructor, and he thinks I should be ready for some serious dives in a few more days." I put on a straight face and tried to sound very confident.

"Just be careful, huh." He looked a little concerned.

"Plan to." We both rose from our chairs at the same time and shook hands.

"Thanks Noah, I really appreciate your help."

"No problem. I'll call you when I have something."

"That'll be great. If you need anymore help on the other thing, let me know."

CHAPTER 17

After Dave left I sat down and blew out a deep breath and did some thinking, *Dave talked about three suspects, but he only mentioned one. Valentine. Could Sean Kilbane be one of them? He made several trips to Buffalo. Unwarranted trips according to Mark Richter, his boss. And what about Hank, his Mark V came out of Canada, and I think his XKE did too. But Sean didn't buy any cars out of Canada. He only had the one car. The Lincoln, and he got that from his Dad. Was that true? And what about Hank? He told me he bought his Mark V from some guy in Canada. Was he lying? As I recall Hank's Jaguar "E" type came from a guy in Toronto. Was the Jag one of the six cars Dave talked about? Questions, questions. I can't believe any of this. For one thing Hanks too smart to get himself mixed up in anything like this. He worked to hard to get where he's at, the youngest bank President in the state. Actually there was one younger, in a small town down state, but the guy's father owns the bank. So that doesn't count. So who else in the club bought cars out of Canada? I hadn't heard.*

Who else in the club acquired a car in the last eight months. There were a few, at least three, maybe four. But these were all men of means. Prominent citizens of the community. I think Dave's all wet. I don't think his theory holds water. We're talking about some low life's, nobody in the club fits that description.

The best I can do is prove to Dave that he's wrong. Tony Valentine is a wealthy developer. He lives in Gates Mills, comes from a wealthy family. I really think Dave is reaching. I was struggling with my thoughts when the phone rang, it startled me.

"Noah?" It was Monica.

"Yeah. Hi hon."

"I was dozing. The phone startled me." I lied.

"Did you forget?"

"What?" My head was still unclear.

"You were going to pick me up. Our lesson. We have a lesson tonight. Remember."

"Yeah sure, I remember. What time is it?" As I looked at my watch.

"It's almost 5:30." she said, a little miffed.

"Oops. I'll be right over." I hung up grabbed my gear bag and rushed down to the garage. This would be our last private lesson, and it was going very well. Monica took to scuba diving with ease. She was a natural. Good lungs, strong legs and a kind of sixth sense. She was totally aware of her surroundings at all times. She remembered all the pit falls of deep diving. I on the other hand tended to wander. I was short on concentrating, big on wandering. The basic diving techniques were no problem. I knew how to work the equipment. I should have no problem diving on my own. I just had to pay better attention to my surroundings.

We had been warned that one of the pitfalls of diving on a ship wreck was to get too excited and forget about your surroundings. That could be very dangerous. I was glad Monica was my diving partner. She was cool, calm and collected, not easily distracted.

146

We had decided that after today's lesson, we would practice on our own. Max agreed to be our charter captain, seeing as he had the boat. There were a couple of well known ship wrecks off the lighthouse at Lorain harbor, at the mouth of the Black River. One was at twenty feet and the other at thirty feet. This would be very good practice. So, over the next four days, weather permitting, we would make our practice dives. Then if all goes well, on the last weekend in June, again weather permitting, we would dive on the Alice Good. It would be our only opportunity before the July forth weekend and our car show.

I decided not to take a car to the show. Not having a car would give me more mobility, a little more freedom, and relaxation. Monica was a little surprised at my decision, but she didn't question it. We were going to drive over to the show with Denise and Hank on Friday. Monica asked Mora if she would like to join us, but she declined, her parents were coming to town.

CHAPTER 18

Wednesday morning as I was getting ready to leave, the phone rang. I hesitated, I thought about letting the machine answer it, but on the third ring I picked up.

"Noah. Can you bug out today?" It was Max.

"I guess I could get away. What's up?"

"It's a beautiful day I thought we could head up to Vermilion, take a shake down cruise."

"Sounds tempting. I'll need to make a phone call." I didn't
need much convincing, it was a beautiful day.

"Aw right! Make the call, I'll pick you up in thirty minutes."
'click', he broke the connection. A man of few words. No
nonsense. It's what I like about Max.

I called my dad at the job site, gave him a lame excuse, and
promised to have his supplies at the loft first thing in the morning.
Then I called Monica and filled her in. She said it wasn't fair. I
promised to make it up to her. No sooner had I hung up, the
downstairs buzzer sounded. I looked at my watch, thirty minutes
and Max was here. I grabbed the manila envelope with the Xerox
copy of the old chart, Alice Good info and my note book, and
headed downstairs.

The drive out to Vermilion took about forty minutes. Max drove
his 1948 Chrysler Town and Country convertible. It's a large,
heavy car. The car is often referred to as Americas Land Yacht .
The body is made of white ash with mahogany panels. Weighs
about two tons and is powered by an inline eight cylinder engine,
coupled to a fluid drive transmission. Requires the same
maintenance as a wood boat. It's a fantastic road car. Big and
comfortable, the ride is soft. The top was down, the sun and warm
breeze made for a perfect trip. We didn't say to much, and I
thoroughly enjoyed the ride.

Max owns a twenty-seven foot Wellcraft. The name of the boat
is 'Columbine'. According to Max it's his one claim to fame.
While serving in the Air Force, he filled in as co-pilot for one flight
on Air Force One. To commemorate that event and honor
Eisenhower, his favorite president, he named the boat after

Eisenhower's Air Force One, which was called 'Columbine'. It's the Kansas state flower, Ike's home state.

After removing the mooring cover, Max primed and started the engine, then turned on the bilge pump. I made myself useful by carrying the picnic cooler from the car to the boat. It contained sandwiches and beer.

We undid the lines and headed down the river to the open waters of Lake Erie. It takes about 20 minutes to reach the lake, traveling at idle speed. Once we were out of the break wall, Max leaned on the throttle, the tachometer moved up to 3500 RPM, we were cruising on a northwest course for the islands.

Ten minutes out Max set the boat on auto pilot. He came aft, opened the cooler and retrieved a couple of beers, handing one to me. Comfortably settled, he took a long swig and set the bottle in a cup holder.

"I dug up a couple of things on our friend Mickey, want to hear?" He asked.

"Sure, go ahead."

"First off, he has an alibi of sorts for the day your friend was killed. But, it doesn't hold up. He was gone for little more than an hour from the bar."

"Oh yeah." He had my attention.

"His afternoon man offered that up for twenty bucks. He was gone between 7:00 and 8:00 that night. I also did some checking at the hall of records. Seems our buddy is in debt up to his eyeballs. Mortgaged to the hilt. And, word on the street is he's in to some bookie for a small bundle. His bar business does well but he likes to bet on his old team."

"The Browns didn't do very well last season." I offered.

"Exactly. And that my friend may add up to a motive. As I see it, Mickey probably offered Sean the use of his boat and his diving skills for a piece of the action. But he gets a little greedy, they have a confrontation, and Mickey pops 'em."

"Works for me." I said, agreeing with the scenario.

"Yeah, and all we need is a little proof." He finished his beer and went forward to check on the course heading. "Holding a steady 295 degrees. Should be there in half hour. How about another beer?"

"Sure, why not." I walked over to the cooler and dug out a cold Michelob. Then settled into an aft seat, out in the sun, enjoying the wind and the spray.

Max checked the controls and consulted his chart. I drank my beer and thought about Mickey Kilbane. *All I needed was proof. But how was I going to get it? It seems like Mickey has the motive and the opportunity, all I need to do is place him at the scene. I needed a plan.* I got up and went forward to the bridge and peered through the windshield. On the horizon the islands were coming into view. I turned to Max, "If Mickey killed Sean, then he has to have the chart."

"That would follow," replied Max.

"So having that chart in his possession would put him at the scene."

"Probably." Max confirmed.

"Where do you suppose he'd keep it?" It was more of a thought out loud than a question."

"As I see it, you've got your pick of three places" Max offered.

"Right. His home, his boat, where's the third? I asked.

"The bar."

"Right, the bar." Why didn't I think of that. "Max, we have to find that chart."

"I'm all ears." He said.

"Here's what I propose. You shadow Mickey for a few days. See if he established a routine, generally see what he's up to. Based on your info I'll figure a way to get in his house, for a good look around. I'll also check out his boat. More than likely it's on the boat or in his house. I think we can eliminate the bar, too many people have access."

"So you're proposing a clandestine operation."

"Absolutely. You in?"

"Wouldn't miss it." He smiled.

We were heading up the east cost of Kelley's Island, I checked my notes. Max gradually brought the boat around to 280 degrees and headed for the R-4 buoy as indicated in my notes and what was circled on the old chart. We dropped anchor one half mile south of R-4. Gull Island was on our right and Kelley's Island on the left. Max played out the anchor line 60 feet before it caught hold. To the west you could see South Bass Island and Middle Bass Island. The boat traffic was very light. Most of what was there, was between South Bass and the west coast of Kelley's. Max killed the engine. We relaxed.

"Time for lunch." Max announced.

We went into the cabin, sat down at the table. Max broke out the baloney sandwiches and beer. Max is not what you would call a gourmet, baloney sandwiches are his favorite food.

"Where do you figure the Alice Good went down?" asked Max.

I took Xerox copies out of a large envelope, I brought along, and spread them out on the table.

"According to the newspaper accounts of September 29th, 1941, the Alice Good would have been headed in a easterly direction. A storm brewed most of that day and into the night of the 28th . I figure she would have been blown off this spot as she sank", I pointed to a spot on a copy of the old chart.

"And this is the spot that was marked on the original chart?" Max pointed to the location at which we were anchored.

"Right. As near as I can figure there was no damage to the ship. No distress calls were made. And if this ties into the train robbery, as I think it does, then gold was on board and she was scuttled." I pulled out a photo and a cross sectional drawing of the lake freighter from my envelope.

"What have we here?" Asked Max.

"I picked this up at the marine archives at Bowling Green University. It's a photo of the Alice Good, and a diagram of her sister ship. Lets say she was scuttled, then it was probably done in the engine room." I pointed to the aft section of the freighter. "If you look closely, the valves to the ballasts are here and here, also the sea cocks, here and here."

"One man could have done the job." Max remarked, as we studied the diagram. "If that's the way it was done, then she sank stern first."

"Probably. Which means she slipped westward, as she sunk. So she could be as much as a mile or more off this spot." I pointed to the chart.

"Unless the anchor was dropped." Max offered.

Max got up and retrieved a current chart for the south shore of Lake Erie and the islands. He spread it out on the table and compared it to my Xerox copy.

"The current chart shows depth of sixty feet and forty feet in this area." Max made a circle with his finger. "The old chart shows a continuous depth of sixty feet for the same area. Allowing for silt buildup and a change in the water datum, the current lake depth being 3 feet above the water datum, my guess would be that she lies here." He pointed to a spot with his finger.

"Seems about right." I agree.

"Let's check it out," he said. "We can use the depth finder and run a crisscross grid and take some soundings."

"That sounds good to me."

I pulled up the anchor while Max fired up the 'Columbine'. Using the R-4 buoy as a reference point, we headed west on a course heading of 270, for one half mile, then swung around and headed east on a heading of 090. We did this about eight times spacing our runs about two or three yards apart, taking constant depth readings, which were printed out on a continuous sheet.

When we completed our east west runs, we lined up once more on the R-4 buoy and made the same runs north and south, thus giving us a crisscross grid. When the grid was completed Max stopped the boat and turned off the engine. The boat drifted while we checked the depth findings.

From the R-4 buoy heading west, the depth was sixty feet, then it jumped up to thirty-five feet, and back down again to forty feet for a distance of three hundred feet, then it jumped up again to thirty-two feet, then down again to sixty feet.

"What do you think?" I asked.

"I think that's it." said Max, pointing to the depth readings. He looked again at the current chart and laid out an area in pencil. "As you can see the depth is constant then it gets erratic and then gets constant again. Where the reading jumps up here," he pointed, "this has got to be the bow, and the readings we're getting is probably from the wheel house. Notice how they level out then go up again. I think this is the deck, then it rises again at the stern. That's got to be it." He said.

"So you think she's sitting upright!"

"I'd say so." Replied Max. "The north south readings seem to confirm it."

We were a little over two miles north of Kelley's Island and about eighteen hundred yards south of Gull Island, one half mile west of the original mark.

"This should be our dive spot." I indicated a spot on the chart.

"Yup, I'd say that should put you right on the money. No pun intended." Replied Max. "We should take a look at Gull Island as a possible base of operations. What's say we mosey on over and check it out."

"Why not."

Max fired up the engine and we headed over to Gull Island, aiming for a small inlet. We noticed a small dock, a boat house and through the trees you could see a cottage. There were no other boats around. We tied up to the small dock and headed for the cottage. There was no sign of any occupants. A screened porch ran across the cottage front. We opened the screen door and stepped on to the porch. There was a typed sheet inside a three by five frame covered with glass. It hung next to the cottage door and read, "For rental information call: Marvin Holmes at 419-555-0506, Sandusky, Ohio". I jotted down the number on the back of a gas receipt and we headed back to the boat.

"I'll give this guy a call when we get back to Vermillion, check on availability for a week or two. That should give us enough time."

"If you find anything down there when do you think you'll start salvage operations?" asked Max.

"As soon as we confirm the find, I'll contact a salvage company. Hopefully we can start operations immediately." I replied.

"What about this Mickey thing. When do you plan on putting that operation into motion?"

"If the dive proves successful this weekend, then we'll move on that right away. Like on Monday. We'll be out here Friday, Saturday and Sunday, so if he comes sniffing around, that'll pretty much confirm my suspicions. But we'll still have to place him at the scene and finding that chart would do it." This was my plan.

Max headed the 'Columbine' southeast toward one of our proposed dive sites. It took about thirty minutes. We took some soundings and marked the chart accordingly. "This is where we'll begin our dive on Friday." I indicated to the marked spot on the chart.

"You're the boss." replied Max, as he swung the boat easterly and headed for Vermilion.

"Monica will be leaving work early, so we should be in Vermilion by 4:30 PM . How does that work for you?" I asked.

"No problem. I'll be out here earlier in the day, you want me to pick up your dive tanks?"

"That would be great. Save a lot of time. I'd like to get in as much daylight as we can."

"What size tanks do you want?" Asked Max.

"Get four, forty-five minute tanks. Two we'll use on Friday, and two we'll keep as spares."

"You got it." He replied.

"If everything goes as planned we should be done with our dive by 7:00 PM." I said confidently.

"Good, then we can have a not so late dinner at MacGarvey's. I'm buying." Max commanded.

"I'll be looking forward to it. We both will." It would be my chance to make up to Monica for today, even if it was Max's treat.

After the 'Columbine' was docked and secured I headed over to the marina office and called the number in Sandusky. Mr. Holmes explained that the cottage on Gull Island rented for five hundred a week, but if we were interested in two weeks back to back, he would give us a break. Two weeks for nine hundred. I got his address and told him the check would be in the mail and to reserve the cottage for two weeks starting the following Monday. He indicated that I could pick up the key at the South Shore Marina in East Harbor. I advised Max. He would take care of the key and the provisions.

CHAPTER 19

Our practice dive went well. Visibility at the twenty foot level was very good, and at the thirty foot level it wasn't bad either, but we could have used a little more light at times. For our dive on

Friday we decided to carry flashlights and a head lamp. The head lamp is attached to a band that clamps to your head, it leaves your hands free. The flashlights would be our back up.

Monica left work early on Friday and I picked her up at 3:00 PM. She was wearing pink shorts, an extra large T-shirt that read: "Run America March of Dimes" over her bathing suit, and tan deck shoes. I loaded her gear in with mine.

"Pretty day," she said getting into the car.

"Very". I replied. "According to "NOEL Weather Radio", the National Weather Service for Lake Erie, the South Shore and the islands. "Wind was from the southwest at five to ten knots, and waves were one to two feet. Can't get any better than that."

"We should have no problems." She said, with a good deal of confidence.

"I agree, it should be perfect."

"Did you get the tanks recharged?" She asked.

"Max is handling that." I said. "Knowing Max, they should already be on the boat."

"I like Max." She mused. "He's charming, calm, efficient, knowledgeable, very capable, and good to have around."

"Enough already. Max is a good guy, I agree." She gave me a look.

The drive took forty minutes. We pulled into the parking area and headed for slip number forty-five. Max had the 'Columbine' all loaded and ready to go.

"No food or drink till after our dive." It was a general statement. Max and Monica already knew this , so I was ignored, as they went about their business. *"Well that was a little foolish", I thought. "Oh well so much for establishing my authority".*

We were underway for almost an hour, when Monica asked, "How much longer to the dive site?"

"About fifteen minutes." Answered Max.

Monica removed her shorts, T-shirt and deck shoes. She slipped on her dive boots. The temperature was seventy-four and was headed for a high of eighty-five. The water temperature was at seventy-four degrees Fahrenheit. It would be warm enough, but we opt to wear wet suits, boots and gloves, only because we didn't know what we'd run into. If you scraped your hand or foot, or any part of your body on something rusty or even a shell, it could cause an infection. The clothing we would be wearing should guard against such an occurrence. Monicas' wet suit was hot pink and lavender over black. She looked like an ad for the wet suit manufacturer. The skin tight suit highlighted every curve of her body. She looked fantastic. I noticed Max watched her with a big smile on his face.

Taking my "Q" from Monica, I stripped down to my bathing trunks and put on my wet suit. My suit was safety yellow over black. We checked out each others equipment. Flash light, head lamp, depth gauge, air gauge, compass, and dive watch. As we approached the dive site , we put on our BC's (it's a type of vest, a buoyancy compensator. It allows you to vary your buoyancy under water. It connects to your air supply and breathing apparatus. Helps to control your ascent and supports you at the surface. An indispensable piece of equipment.) Next we put on our swim fins and weight belts.

Once he had the engine stopped and the anchor deployed, Max helped us with our air tanks. We each had forty-five minute tanks. The plan was, to dive and try to locate the wreck in thirty minutes or less. If we did not locate the Alice Good in thirty minutes we would surface and get fresh tanks. The fifteen minutes was a safety margin. Max had acquired four sets of tanks. Even if we located the ship in the thirty minutes, our exploring of the ship would be done with fresh tanks.

We were ready to go. We each fixed our hoods and dipped our masks in water before securing them in place. Max helped with the head lamps. We cleared our mouth pieces and checked the flow of air. I gave a thumbs up and we both entered the water simultaneously from either side of the boat.

Once in the water, we cleared our masks, made our final adjustments, and dove for the bottom. When we reached 30 feet we deployed a SMB (surface marker buoy) and Monica played out a line as we followed the anchor rope to the bottom. The SMB would let Max know where we were at all times.

Visibility was very good, even at the thirty foot level. It became a little murky at fifty feet. Checking our depth guage we leveled off and headed southwest. A few Walleye swam along with us. We swam for about ten minutes when our head lamps picked up a large, dark and foreboding image. As we got closer it got larger and took on the shape of a ships' bow. It was eerie, we were dwarfed by its size. The Alice Good may have been a small ship by lake freighter standards, but sitting in sixty feet of dark water it was a giant. A cold chill ran down my spine. It sat upright, as Max had predicted, with a slight list to starboard. It was covered with layers of zebra mussels. Little creatures that had invaded the great lakes in the last few years, by way of ocean going vessels from Europe,

You could barely make out the name painted on her side. But there was no mistaking her. It was the Alice Good. We made our way to the wheelhouse, shining our lights inside. All the window glass was missing. Monica checked her watch and air gauge. She pointed at me and gave a thumbs up. It was time to surface. We attached a line to a window frame and played out another SMB of a different color then our first one. We followed that line upward adjusting our BC's as we rose.

We broke the surface about fifty yards from the boat. We signaled to Max. He raised the anchor and steered the boat toward us at idle speed. When he was close he cut the engine and deployed the anchor. Letting the boat drift to us. We swam to the stern swim platform. I pulled down the ladder, Monica exited first. Then I followed, tossing my fins on deck before climbing aboard.

"Well?" Max said. Looking at both of us for a response.

"It's down there Max. Big as life. It's there." I said, trying to contain my excietment.

"Hot damn." He acknowledged, with a big smile. Then he took a cigar out of his pocket and lit up. Satisfaction written all over his face.

"It's going to take a couple more dives to explore the whole ship." I said. "We'll rest for thirty minutes then dive again." Max helped with the spent tanks.

Thirty minutes later, with fresh tanks, we were in the water diving on the Alice Good. We followed the SMB line down and deployed another SMB so Max could track our movement.

The first place we explored was the wheel house. Then some of the quarters. Most of the wood trim had rotted away. Some of the compartments we could not get into because the doors would not open. I had expected to find skeletons of the crew members. There were none. *I speculated about this, what could have happened to them? Did they actually leave the ship and subsequently drown? Like the two skeletons that were found in the old skiff off Lakside.*

One of the hazards of diving on a ship wreck is silt. Silt is everywhere, on every surface. It could be a very thin layer, or a few feet thick. Silt is made up of particulate matter, caused by rusting metal and microbial destruction of organic matter, such as wood from the ships furniture and wood trim. Window and door frames, paneling, etc. It covers walls, floors and ceilings. The least agitation can send up a cloud. Enough agitation could plunge you into total darkness, causing disorientation. Because there is no current inside a wreck, it could take hours for the silt to settle.

We had about ten minutes of air left and decided to check out the stern section, which housed the galley and more of the crews quarters. Again all the window glass was missing, their frame long ago rotting away. We shown out lights into the galley. Something in the corner of the room caught my eye. It was partially visible, buried in the silt. Looked like a giant egg. My first thought a giant turtle egg. But not in Lake Erie. The doorway was clear, so I went in. I reached for the object, but it was stuck. I pulled, it came loose, and I dropped it in the silt, causing a small cloud. Monica played her flashlight on me as I went to retrive the object. I reached down and as soon as I touched it I released it, backing away, as a silt cloud bellowed from the deck. It was a human

162

skull. It sent cold shivers down my spine, and even though we were in fifty feet of water, I broke out in a cold sweat. I actually felt clammy.

I retreated though the doorway. Monica saw the look on my face and was concerned. She checked her watch and gave me a thumbs up. I shook my head affirmatively and we followed the SMB line to the surface.

Once on board I removed my head lamp, mask and hood. Shrugged off my tank as quickly as I could. Took a deep breath and sat on the deck, arms wrapped around my knees. It was eighty-five degrees and I was cold.

"What's the matter with you?" Asked Max. "You look like you've seen a ghost."

"I guess I did." I mumbled.

"What Happened?"

"Nothing much, I picked up a skull and it scared the shit out of me." I blurted out. "I was expecting to see skeletons, but when I actually did, it shook me up. Go figure."

"Only natural," said Max. "You'll get over it. What's say you take a little longer break before giving it another shot." It was almost noon.

"Okay, let's take a lunch break, " I said. "We can give it another try in about an hour or so. How's that sound to you Monica?"

"Good. I am getting a little hungry." She said.

"You know Max we should have gotton a couple of sixty minute tanks, I miscalculated. Thirty minutes isn't giving us enough time."

"Tell you what," said Max, "we've got a couple of the partially spent tanks with fifteen minutes of air in them. Let's see if I can transfer that into the forty-five minute tanks."

"Do you think you could do it?" I asked.

"I'll give it a shot and let you know."
While Monica and I ate our lunch, Max rigged up the two partially spent tanks and successfully transferred the air into the forty-five's. We now had two one hour tanks for our next dive.

CHAPTER 20

One half mile away a blue and white Bayliner lay at anchor. The lone occupant was glued to a pair of high power binoculars. He was very interested in what was taking place on the 'Columbine'. After a while he lowered the glasses and made some notes. Then took up the watch once more.

Before we made our next dive, we consulted the diagram of the freighter. Laying out a dive plan so we could conserve air. The plan was simple and direct. We strapped on our tanks and made ready for our water entry. Once in the water Monica and I joined up and followed the SMB line down to the ghostly ship.

Once we disappeared into our dive, Max made his way inside the cabin. He had been aware of the Bayliner. He retrieved a pair of high power Navy surplus field glasses and focused on the Bayliner. By staying inside the cabin he put himself out of view to any curious onlookers. As he suspected, the Bayliner was keeping us under surveillance. Although he could not make out the facial features, he noted that the lone figure on the Bayliner was male, tall, with a athletic build. The party on the Bayliner was either a curious spectator, or an active player. Which one he could only guess.

As part of our dive plan, we decided that if the gold was on board, it was most likely put there with the help of the ships crane, or cargo boom. Loading sixteen hundred pounds of gold by hand would have taken a very long time and might have raised some suspicion. So the most logical place would be the cargo holds. There were four. All the hatches were open, which aided in scuttling the ship. We would have to explore each of the cargo holds, one at a time.

The plan was, that one of us would go indside the hold while the other remained at the opening. We would deploy a tether line between us and take turns.

I was apprehensive, but elected to explore the first hold. *I told myself, the sooner we do this the sooner we'll be out of here. This was not turning into a fun dive.* I signaled to Monica that I was ready. She nodded her head and played out our tether line. I turned, made a strong kick and entered the hold.

Monica played her light into the hold after me. I descended head first, into the black hole. I kept playing my light from side to side, top to bottom. I had just about reached bottom when something

165

slapped the back of my head. Startled, I turned with a quick motion, my feet went down and I was almost in a standing position. I played the light behind me, and caught a glimpse of what looked like a two foot long Walleye. The quick motion of my fins agitated the silt, creating a large silt cloud, it cut my visibility drastically. I panicked, made another sharp turn. Creating another silt cloud, now I had no visibility. I was like a trapped fish, trashing around, making matters worse. The cold sweat and fear set in.

"Which way is up? I can't see. How much air do I have left? How long will it take for the cloud to subside? Shit, it could take hours! I didn't have enough air! What do I do?" With all this racing through my mind I felt a tug on the tether line. Monica! Thank God.

From the time I had entered, Monica had shone her light into the hold and watched my progress. But with the thick silt cloud I couldn't see it. She saw my predicament and began tugging on the line. It snapped me out of my panic and I slowly rose up the line, while she took in the slack. As I got to the hold opening, I finally saw her light. The cloud continued to bellow out of the hold and began to dissipate as it rose.

We swam a few yards away and stopped. I checked my air gauge while she checked hers, we had thirty minutes of air left. Monica gave me the thumbs up signal to rise to the surface. I shook it off pointing to my air gauge. She nodded that she understood. We had plenty of time. So we swam over to the stern, to hold number four. Keeping two holds and the silt cloud between us.

Once we reached the opening to hold number four, she handed me the tether spool. I undid the line from my weight belt and passed it to her, which she fastened to her belt. Once the line was

166

secure, she gave me an "OK" sign and dove into the blackness of the hold.

I played my light after her and watched her descend. She did so slowly, trying not to disturb or agitate the silt. The flash light and head lamp were good for maybe fifteen to twenty feet. With my light playing into the hold and hers inside the hold, I began to make out a mass of some kind on the floor of the hold. I could just about make out her swimming around, playing her light on the mass. After awhile she stopped at one end of the mass, moving her light around one spot.

Ten minutes later she came up. When she reached the top of the hold, she indicated that she wanted to ascend. You could see the excitement in her eyes. We swam to the surface.

Once on board the 'Columbine' Max helped us out of our gear, and we all sat around the cabin table. "Noah. Max. It is down there." It was a simple, straight forward statement.

"You mean the gold?" I said.

"Yes. The gold. It is inside an old truck."

"No shit!" Said Max.

"There is more." She said. "Someone else has been here."

"How do you know?" I asked.

"The gold is in wooden boxes, or what is left of them. It looks like two bars in each box. The remnants of the boxes that were close to the truck door are empty. The bars are gone."

167

"Do you think this happened recently?" Asked Max.

"The way the wood remnants are scattered about, I would say it was recent." She replied.

"Then we've got to move fast. I guess my buddy Mickey didn't waste any time." I was on my feet.

"What's your plan kiddo?" Asked Max.

"We go down one more time and bring up a bar or two. It leaves Mickey a message, that we're on to him. Probably force his hand. Next I notify Mora, she can amend the salvage application to reflect the actual cargo. Then I contact a salvage company and make the necessary arrangements." I was pacing around the cabin as I spoke. Max and Monica were still seated. "Max how's our air supply?"

"Let me check." Max rose and went out on deck to take inventory.

"Noah, what will you do with the gold?" Monica asked.

"Let Mora have it. I believe it's rightfully her's. It was Sean who found the chart in the first place. Anyway it's small compensation for a man's life."

"Good." She said, getting up and giving me a great big kiss. "Noah, I love you." She turned and walked out on deck.

"You've got about thirty minutes all total." Was Max's assessment of our air supply.

"Not enough." I said.

"I'll drop you two at Gull Island, then make a run to the mainland for refills."

"Great. We've got our SMB out there, so no problem finding this spot, and we can keep an eye on the site from the island."

We stowed our gear, weighed anchor and headed for Gull Island. Monica and I had changed into our shorts before we reached the dock.

"Max did you get the key to the cottage?"

"Picked it up yesterday." He handed me the key. "Stocked up the place with grub and drink, all the comforts of home."

"Max, you are a helluva guy. Helluva guy." I embellished. "How long do you think for the round trip?"

"Couple of hours, give or take."

"Noah, we should wait till tomorrow to make another dive." Said Monica.

"Exactly my thoughts. No use pushing it. Take your time Max, we'll do the dive tomorrow."

Max looked at Monica then winked at me, as I cast off the lines. As he headed south away from the island, Max paid special attention to the area where the blue and white Bayliner was anchored. It was gone. Apparently departing sometime during the last dive. *"That was good", he thought, "The integrity of our base camp was still intact."*

Monica and I made love on the sofa bed inside the warm cottage, a single oscillating fan blowing warm air over our bodies. I dosed off. Monica rose and showered. Max got back around 5:00 PM.

"We're all set for tomorrow." He announced.

"Perfect. I could use a beer. How about you."

"Yeah, sure."

"Monica you want one?"

"Yes, sounds good."

We sat on the screened porch sipping our beers, watching the boats on the lake. We had an excellent vantage point. The cottage was hidden from view while out on the lake. But from the cottage the lake view was excellent, with a very good view of the dive site.

"By the way," Max leaned forward in his chair, "I got us a back up for the boat. An inflatable skiff with a twenty-five HP outboard. I got it tied at the dock."

"How in the world did you come up with that?" I was impressed. This was a great idea.

"Guy at the marina rents them. So I thought why not." He took a swig of beer and emptied his bottle.

"Why not indeed." We all laughed.

"By the way, what's the weather for tomorrow?" I asked.

"NOEL Weather say's pretty much a repeat of today. Swells one to two feet, building three to four by early afternoon. Wind five to ten at two zero five, clear skys, fifteen to twenty thousand broken, ten mile visibility, with a high of eighty-five degrees."

"Perfect day. We should get an early start." I suggested.

"How about some supper?' Asked Max. "You fire up the grill and I'll put on some hot dog's. Monica you can break out the chips and dip."

"I'm hungry."

"Me too."

We set about doing our assigments, the sun was going down, the sky turned orange to red, and there was a light breeze. As the saying goes, "red sky at night, sailors delight". Fitting end to a rewarding day.

Monica and I shared the sofa bed, Max strung a hammock on the porch. Max set the clock in his head, he would be up early and get us going. Tomorrow was going to be a busy day.

Max had breakfast cooking early. He made eggs, sausage, hash browns, toast and coffee. Monica and I had a light breakfast, one egg, toast and coffee. We departed the dock at 8:00 AM. It only took a few minutes to reach the dive site.

Before we dove we agreed to enter the hold together and try to retrive at least two of the bars. Max found us a plastic bucket, which we would take with us. A line was tied to the bucket, we would load the bars in the bucket and Max would pull them to the surface, we would follow behind supporting the bucket.

We entered the hold as agreed, the plan was to avoid sudden movements, stay off the bottom, and keep away from the sides. Minimize any silt cloud. When we reached the truck, we moved as if in slow motion. Making deliberate moves. Monica played her light on the truck and cargo, while I tried to retrieve one of the bars. The bar was covered in slime and silt, it was hard to grasp. It took a couple of tries before I managed to get one of the bars into the bucket. No matter how hard we tried, we were creating a silt cloud and visibility was going to be a problem. Monica gave a thumbs up, I agreed. One bar was better than none. We give a tug on the bucket line, Max began to pull, we followed behind, supporting the bucket all the way to the surface.

Once on board the 'Columbine' we got out of our dive suits and closely examined the gold bar. When it was cleaned up you could make out the name of the mining company and a smelting number.

"Sixteen pounds of gold. What do you think it's worth?" asked Max.

"According to Fridays Plain Dealer, gold closed at nine hundred and forty-three dollars an ounce. So roughly, I'd say this baby is worth about (I did some rough calculating rounding off), over two hundred thousand dollars."

He let out a whistle, "what are you going to do with it?"

"For now we'll just put it into the picnic cooler." I walked over to the cooler, raised the lid, took out three cold beers and slid the bar inside.

We marked our chart as to the exact location and removed the SMB. Then pulled up anchor and headed back to Gull Island.

"Not a bad mornings work", very pleased with myself. My thoughts then turned to Mickey. He would have had a difficult time getting the bars by himself. Unless he had help, or some sort of wench set-up. But what he had recovered, if found in his possession would be very incriminating.

After lunch we planned out strategy. Max indicated that on his previous surveillance of Mickey he noted that Mickey was busy at the bar on Mondays. The day most of his deliveries arrived and he had to be there. This would be a perfect time for me to search his boat. We still needed to put him in Sean's house the night of the murder. Monica did not like what we were planing and voiced her concerns in no uncertain terms. However, without an alternative, she reluctantly agreed.

When we returned home, I would call Mora and let her know what we had found. Then on Monday I would contact a salvage company and make the necessary arrangements.

Plans for the upcoming July fourth weekend I left to Monica. Reservations at the hotel were already made, but she had to coordinate times with Denise and Hank, since they were doing the driving. I still had that thing to do for Kaminski and I had no clue as to how I would get that accomplished. My dad was not going to be a happy camper. We were nearing completion on the loft job and I was not going to be around. *"Somehow I'd make it up to him." I told myself. "I'd work it out."*

CHAPTER 21

It was 8:00 PM when I made my way up the stairs to the apartment. I checked my machine, no messages. After stowing my gear, I dialed Mora's number. She picked up on the second ring. She had just returned from the airport, after dropping off her parents. I told her about the success of our dive in finding the gold. Her reaction was passive. I didn't know how she would react to the news, but I did not figure on dead silence.

I further explained that the gold was rightfully hers, in as much as it was Sean who discovered the chart. More silence. I explained that after reviewing my notes, it would not be necessary for her to amend the salvage application since the original application indicted precious metal. I figured it would be better if we were not specific. More silence.

Then after a long pause she told me how much she appreciated our efforts, mine and Monica's, and for believing in her. She said she was not ungrateful, but somehow the gold seemed unimportant, and did I understand. I said I did.

"I'm sure Sean would have been pleased." I added.

"Yes, I'm sure he would have been." She said with a little difficulty. It was still hard for her to accept all that had happened.

"Look, I'll take care of lining up a salvage company and we'll get started as soon as possible."

I explained about the two missing bars and for the urgency for proceeding quickly. I told her about my thoughts on Mickey's envolvment and that we still needed proof.

"I am going to try my best in doing just that." I said.

"You know he called here again, just the other day." She said.

"Really! What for?" I asked, somewhat surprised.

"To see how I was getting along, and if there was anything he could do for me. He really sounded sincere."

"Bastard has gaul, I'll give him that."

"You really think he did it?" She asked, not convinced.

"Everything points that way. Motive and opportunity. And all I have to do is place him at the scene, then I go to the cops."

"You know best." She said, without any real conviction.

"I'll keep you posted." We said our goodbyes and she clicked off. I sat there for a minute thinking about Mickey. "I wonder what his game is? What was the real reason for his calling Mora?"

Monday morning came quickly, it was 8:00 AM. I looked up a salvage company based in Sandusky, "Slate and Sons, Marine Salvage, 30 years Experience" the ad read. Joseph Slate answered the phone. I found out later that he was the younger of the two son's. I explained the job to him, without divulging the actual cargo.

"I'm interested in only salvaging the cargo." I repeated.

"Okay. Now what is the cargo?" He asked, for a second time.

"Artifacts, heavy metal, parts of an old truck. Approximately 1600 pounds."

"You're sure of the location?" Double checking.

"Yes, we dove on the wreck just this weekend. I've got it marked on the chart and there will be a SMB at the site." I assured him.

"And you do have a salvage permit?"

"Yes."

"Our operation is simple. We use a salvage tug, and at least two divers. Bottom suction equipment for the silt and in this case a wench and basket. The rate is fifteen hundred dollars per hour, portal to portal. Operation like this, probably take eight to ten hours. We'll need a two hour deposit."

"That's fine. I'll have the money to you tomorrow. How soon can you start?"

"Well now there's a problem. Won't be able to get to it much before a week from Wednesday. Weather permiting we can start on that day."

"Is that the best you can do?"

"Afraid so."

"Tell you what. There's a fifteen hundred dollar bonus if you

176

can move up that date."

"Yes sir, I'll do my best." The tone of his voice changed. He was receptive to the bonus. "But we'll need that deposit and a copy of your savage permit and the location."

"You'll have the deposit tomorrow, and the permit and the location on the day you dive.

"That'll be fine. Now you'll be down here tomorrow with the deposit?

Once again I assured him that I would. *"These salvage people are very cautious". I thought. "Must have been stung a few times."*

After my conversation with the salvage company I called Max.
"Max there's been a delay in our plans. The salvage company can't get started till next week. Looks like you're going to have to baby sit the dive site."

"You're the boss." He said.

"They will try to move things up, otherwise it'll be a week from Wednesday. Any problem with this on your end?"

"Nope."

"Good. One more thing. As long as you're going to be in that neighborhood, how about swinging by the salvage company in Sandusky and leave them a deposit."

"I knew there would be more. What's it going to cost me?"

"Three K. Can you swing it? If not I'll meet you at the bank. Oh, and tell them I'll fax the salvage permit."

"Kiddo you're going to owe me a bundle."

I gave him the address of the salvage company, filled him in on my conversation with Joseph Slater and we hung up. It was now 10:00 AM. I was about to leave, when the phone rang. For one second I thought of letting the machine pick up, but then decided against it. It could be Monica or Max.

"You all set for the weekend?" It was Hank.

"Hi Hank. Yeah, I guess. Monica is going to work out the details with Denise. I've been really jammed lately."

"Hey work is supposed to be fun. More avocation than vocation, remember? It's what you always tell us poor office types."

"You're right. It's the extra curricular stuff that keeps getting in the way." I lamely pleaded.
"Right! And how is the investigation going?" He asked.

"Actually pretty good. If everything goes as planned I should be able to nail him in the next few days." I said confidently.

"Nail him? Who?"

"Mickey Kilbane."

"No shit, Mickey Kilbane."

"Yeah, only keep it to yourself. I haven't gone to the cops yet."

178

"No problem. Do you really think it'll stick?" He asked.

"I'm pretty sure. Everything points that way. I should be able to wrap it up in the next few days."

"Keep me posted." He said. "And by the way how's the diving going?"

"Great. We did some this weekend. Perfect weather."

"Yeah it sure was. Where abouts? I mean, where did you do your diving?"

"Up around the islands."

"Great place for diving, find anything interesting?"

"Swam with a school of Walleye. One must have been at least two feet long."

"Sounds like fun."

"It was, tell you all about it this weekend. Hank, I hate to cut this short, but I really got to run."

"Avocation or extra curricular?"

I laughed without replying. "Really got to go."

"Okay my friend, see you Friday."

By the time I rounded the corner onto Clifton, heading for the Edgewater Marina, it was almost 10:30 AM. My morning was slipping by, *"was it already to late? Would there be more people this time of day? Would I have to abort the search?"* All this was *running thought my head as I pulled into the marina parking lot.* While I pondered my situation, another situation was taking place across town in Beechwood.

"Well?" Said a demanding voice on the other end of the phone line, as Tony squirmed in his chair.

"A couple of detectives were here, asked a few questions about the car, and how well I knew Preebe. Took about twenty minutes." Answered Tony.

"What about the car?"

"I got it back on Friday. Cops really messed it up. Then they let it sit in an impound lot , bastards. I got it in a detail shop now getting it cleaned up. Hopefully it'll be ready for the show this weekend."

"What were they looking for?"

"I don't know. Can't figure it out. The only thing I noticed missing was the customs form from the glove box. Can't figure what the hell they would want with that?"

"Tony, you better watch your ass. Make sure you cover everything."

"Shouldn't be a problem. I can't see how they could tie us to Preebe."

"Just watch it. Look, I'll see you this weekend." There was a click and the conversation was over.

The marina parking lot had about a dozen cars, no more. Probably some early fishermen. My luck was holding. I showed Max's Inter-lake Boating Association card to the guard at the gate. He just nodded as I walked out on to the dock area. According to the information Max gave me, Mickey's boat was in slip number 17 on "E" dock. I had no trouble finding 'Barkeeper'. A twenty-four foot blue and white Bayliner.

The boat was nosed into the slip. I checked around the dock area, no one in sight. There was a flap door stitched into the clear plastic mooring cover, I unzipped it with authority. I boarded the boat like it was mine. In case anyone was watching. The layout was familiar, it was a lot like Hank's boat. I've been on Hank's boat many times, enough to know where things were in general. I looked around the deck. Mickey kept a neat boat. Below the bridge was the cabin, there was no lock on the door. "Trusting soul" I thought. The cabin housed a double berth, a galley. A head and shower and an aft berth. There were a number of storage compartments. Methodically I went through them all without results. No chart. I stepped back on deck and went up on the bridge. I checked the compartment along side the wheel. There was a twelve by twelve section of chart covered with an ascetate overlay. It was a current chart for the south shore, including the islands. An area north and west of Kelleys Island was circled with a red grease pencil. It was the general area where we were doing our diving. *"More fingers pointing in his direction, but not proof," I thought.* I was studying the chart when I heard the voices.

"Hi Frank, how did you do? Catch anything?"

"Hi Mickey. Caught a couple of nice Walleye out by the five mile crib." Frank held up his catch.

"Nice, very nice. What did you use?"

"Erie Derie and worms. About twenty-five feet down."

I looked out the windscreen in the direction of the voices. It was Mickey alright. *"Damn! How do I explain this."* Dumb Noah! *This was dumb.* I slipped the chart bach into the compartment. My search was cut short. I got down to the deck and eased out on to the dock, zipped the flap shut. So far, so good.

The boat moored in the adjacent slip was shielding me from view, *but how do I get past Mickey?* As I was contemplating the situation, Mickey ended his conversation, turned and was heading toward his boat. There was only one thing I could do. Quickly and as quietly as I could, I slid off the dock and slipped into the not to clean water.

I tried to keep from swallowing the water, for fear I would start coughing. It was only about five feet deep. I made my way under the dock to the mooring slips on the other side. Then worked my way toward the pier. When I was a safe distance away, I pulled myself up the ladder and on the the swim platform, of a new looking SeaRay. Once on the dock I walked back to the parking lot. Shaking his head, a wry smile on his face, the guard at the gate gave me a curious look.

"What's so funny," I thought. "Like he's never seen anybody dripping wet in street clothes before."

By the time I got back in my Cherokee, Mickey's boat was out in the channel and heading for open water.

182

CHAPTER 22

With my clandestine operation somewhat of a bust, I spent the rest of the week at the job site, much to my dad's surprise. The job was wrapping up, we were applying the finishing touches. Then a final walk through and it's done. This is the part I hate. It seems to drag on forever.

Monica had made arrangments for us to be picked up by Hank and Denise, at the fire station on Friday afternoon. Hank was driving the XJ-6, his daily driver. He had shipped the Mark V Coupe in an enclosed trailer ahead of us. Once we were settled comfortably in Hanks Jag, I thought I'd needle him a little.

"I can't believe you shipped your car!"

"Hell this is a national meet. That baby is going to get a Junior First. You can take that to the bank." He was very serious.

His compulsion for awards and recognition was becoming an obsession. It was a side of Hank I hadn't known. We used to scoff at guys who trailered their cars. Called them wimps. If your car was any good, you drove it and still won. Apparently all that mattered was winning, and he was taking no chances. I was determined to have fun this weekend, so I shrugged off any deep meaning to his actions and just smiled. It was a beautiful afternoon with the weatherman promising lots of sunshine for the entire weekend.

We arrived at the Wavecrest Hotel a little before 4:00 PM. After check-in Monica and Denise elected to soak up the late afternoon sun, while Hank and I decided to check out the bar. We agreed to meet back at our rooms around 6:30 PM, to change for dinner.

Hank and I found a couple of empty seats at the far end of the bar and ordered a couple of Becks. It's Hank's favorite beer. A quick check of the room yielded no familiar faces. Either we were early or the other participants in the weekend activities were taking in any number of hospitality suites. Each chapter and region of the Classic Car Owners Club was sponsoring a hospitality suite. We preferred the bar.

"So how is your pursuit of Mickey Kilbane going?" Asked Hank.

"Not good,"

"Oh yeah, how so?"

"Well, for openers." I took a swallow of beer. "You know that old chart Sean showed us, the night we were at his house?"

"Yeah."

"I think that's the reason he was killed. For that old chart?"

"Are you serious!" Said Hank.

"Very much so. Now hear me out." I outlined my theory. He listened intently and interrupted only to order another round.

"Wow, that's some theory. So you think Mickey's the guy who killed Sean and made off with the chart."

"That's the way I see it. He had the opportunity and the motive. All I need to do is tie him to the scene. Finding that chart in his possession would do it."

"Have you told this to the police?"

"Not yet. I still need the proof. The chart provides the tie in."

"I see your point. Where do you go from here?"

"I guess I'll have to give it another try. Check out his boat one more time." I took another swig of my beer.

"What happens if you find the chart?"

"I'll go to the cops. The rest will be up to them."

"Boy I just can't believe this. Sean murdered for the old chart, and the Mickey Kilbane thing. Sounds so bizarre." Hank finished his beer. "How about another round?"

"Sure, why not." I chugged what was left of my beer and set the empty bottle on the bar and glanced over at the door. More people were entering the bar and one of them was Tony Valentine. He spotted us and headed on over.

"Hi guy's, how's it going?" We shook hands. He was all smiles and as usual was dressed in the latest casual style. Right out of the pages of a J.Crew catalog.

"Pull up a stool and join us." Invited Hank. "Barkeep, a drink for my friend. What are you drinking Tony?"

"Scotch rocks."

"Some of your best single malt for my friend."

"Noah, you bring your Merc?" Asked Tony. He was referring to my Mercedes.

"Nope. Bummed a ride with Hank. Thought I'd sit this one out."

"Too bad. I really enjoy that car of yours. You wouldn't consider selling it?"

"Noah will never part with that Merc," said Hank. He plans to will it to me."

"Right. But he's going to be waiting a long time, I plan on living forever." We all laughed.

We sat at the bar swapping car stories for the better part of an hour. Tony talked about nothing but his newly acquired Packard Convertible. He brought it down for the weekend and couldn't wait to show it.

All the time we were talking I kept thinking about the little task I agreed to do for Kaminski. It made me feel a little uneasy. I just knew Dave was way off base. There was no way Tony could have done what Dave had suggested, and I was going to prove it.

"You and Hank must have struck the mother load in Canada. Seems to be a lot of nice cars up there. I mean you with the Packard and Hank with the Mark V. How did you guy's come up with the leads?" I asked.

"Luck my boy. Pure luck. It was for me anyway." said Tony.

"You want to hear something really weird?" Tony set his glass down on the bar and leaned in. "My Packard was involved in a recent homicide."

"What. Seriously?" I asked.

"Yeah," he took a sip of his drink. "Remember ole' Preebe, the detail guy." Hank and I both nodded our heads. "My car was the last one he worked on. Before he was killed."

"No kidding. I read about that. That was your car ?" I said, trying to sound surprised. And let me tell you, cops have no respect for old cars. It was a mess. I had to have it detailed all over again for this show. " He finished his drink and slid off the bar stool. "Gotta go, see you guy's later." He turned and walked away.

I turned to Hank, "how about that. Tony's car involved in a homicide. That's some story."

"Tony's a nice enough guy, but not to bright." Hank said under his breath,

We sat there in silence for a few more minutes, then I looked at my watch, it was 5:15 PM. "Hey we better go meet the girls."

"Yeah, right." Hank finished his beer and we headed back to our rooms.

When I got back Monica was already showered and dressing for the evening. While I showered and dressed, Monica had made arrangements to meet Denise and Hank in the lobby. We decided to eat at the hotel. They have an excellent seafood menu, which

Monica loves. My love of seafood on the other hand is limited to Lake Erie Walleye done up in a beer batter, or a fast food fish sandwich.

Dinner was relaxing, we lingered over coffee and after dinner drinks. We sat on the veranda watching the sun set. It was turning into a beautiful night. Then for no particular reason we decided to take a walk on the beach. The evening was most enjoyable, it was the perfect start to the weekend.

Tomorrow, Saturday, Hank planned to put finishing touches on his car. I volunteered to help, but first I had a committee obligation. As a member in good standing and since I didn't bring a car, I signed up for the parking committee. The parking committee is responsible for the layout of the show, setting up various judging classes, identifying the parking areas with markers and signs. Then, as the cars arrive we make sure that each car is parked in the correct class. My obligation was to work for the first three hours. Monica and Denise planned to go shopping at the large nearby outlet mall.

On Saturday I got up early, 7:00 AM to be exact. I had to meet with the parking committee at 7:30 AM for a breakfast meeting, coffee and a Danish. The meeting was held in one of two tents set up on the back lawn of the hotel. The Wavecrest Hotel rests on four acres of lush green lawn, with a scattering of very large old oak and tall pine trees at the very tip of Pine Point.

The hotel is a white three story Victorian structure with a spacious veranda that wraps around three sides. Part of the veranda serves the hotel restaurant, and the rest is furnished with white high back wicker rockers and adorandack chairs. It looks like a movie set. You would expect to see ladies strolling the grounds in long flowing pastel dresses, wearing large floppy sun

188

hats and carrying parasols.

Pine Point is a peninsula that stretches up from the city of Sandusky out into the south shore of Lake Erie, and forms the eastern shoreline of Sandusky Bay. The northern most four acres is relegated to the Wavecrest Hotel, and everything south of the hotel forms the Pine Point Amusement Park. Simply known as Pine Point.

Pine Point is a theme park well known throughout Ohio, Indiana, Michigan and western Pennsylvania. You enter the park by way of a causeway, that runs along the eastern side of the peninsula. The same road will take you past the park directly to the Wavecrest. Although the park and the hotel are owned by the same corporation, they are operated independently. Guests of the hotel have a special entrance into the park and are offered a special entrance rate. As a guest of the hotel you are not obligated to purchase entry passes. It's an option.

Pine Point has been in existence since the early 1900's and has gone through tremendous transformation over the years. It's the closest thing the Great Lakes area has to a Disney type park. My folks brought me here as a kid and I have some very fond memories of those summers. I still enjoy the park and I promised Monica we would ride the newest, biggest, roller coaster.

The classes for the show were set up according to pre-set rules. We marked off the areas for each class and began checking in and directing cars to their respective spaces. Two yellow and white striped tents were set up close to the hotel. The smaller of the two was for judges, where they would pick up their judging sheets, get their briefing and turn in their tally's. It also served as the official tabulation tent to determine winners of the various classes. The results would then be revealed at the banquet on Sunday night.

The other, larger tent, was a general purpose tent to check in committee members and volunteers, serve refreshments to volunteers during the course of the day and a continental breakfast for two mornings. It was also the general information tent, the regalia store and where you registered and checked in your car for the show.

I found Hank sitting under a tree next to his car, nursing a cold Becks. The number of empties next to his cooler indicated this was his forth. "How's it going?" I asked, as I approached. At first he didn't acknowledge me. He was in deep thought.

Then he looked up, "Oh, hi Noah, didn't see you. All done with your parking?"

"Yeah, how goes the detailing? What can I do?"

"Not much. How about a beer?"

"First, how about some lunch?"

"Yeah, sure." He said.

"They're serving some hot dogs and burgers over in the big tent, how's that sound?"

"Super!" He pulled himself together and we headed over to the big tent.

"The Mark looks great, what else needs to be done?" I asked.

"All done, except for the trunk."

"Whoa, you have been a busy beaver. Tell you what, let's grab

190

a couple of hot dogs to go and get back to your car. I'll do the trunk, while you take a break."

"Best offer I've had all day. It's a deal."

As promised, I cleaned up the trunk, which wasn't much of a job. Hank gave his approval between gulps of beer. When I had finished, we both sat under the shade of the tree, taking in the warmth of the day, drinking beer and eventually drifting into a nap.

"Hey what's this! I figured you'd be waxing away, not that this old bucket needs anything."

I cracked open my eye's to squint at the sound of the voice. It was Tony Valentine.

"Hey fuck you Valentine. Stay away from my car. Go play with your puke Packard." Hank had raised himself on to his elbows and was slurring his rebuff of Tony.

"My, my, aren't we touchy."

"I think it's the Beck's talking." I said raising to my feet. "Tony do me a favor. There's a car cover in the back seat. Cover the Mark while I see that our friend here gets back to the hotel. A couple of hours sleep and a shower and he'll be as good as new."

"Sure thing." replied Tony. "See you guy's tonight."

"Thanks." I helped Hank to his feet, and without much protest we walked back to the hotel.

I got Hank back to his room where Denise took over. "Let him sleep it off," I said.

"Thanks Noah, I don't know what's gotten into him lately." She put on her best smile and saw me to the door. "We'll see you guy's later."

When I reached my room, Monica was drying her hair and had changed into a pair of khaki shorts. "How was your shopping?" I asked.

"It was fun. There were some really good bargains. Look at the jeans and blouse I got." She pointed to the clothes laying on the bed. I walked over and casually looked at them. "Hey how about going to the park and checking out the new roller coaster?"

"Are you up for it?" She asked.

"Absolutely! You're not trying to back out are you?"

"Are you kidding, lets go!"

The first coaster we rode was the "Eliminator", a corkscrew set-up designed to scramble your brains. Next, it was the "Devil Drop", where you pulled 2-G's in free fall. We finished with the "Terminator", the worlds largest roller coaster, where I almost lost my lunch. Monica on the other hand breezed through them all and would have gone for more, but time was on my side. We had to get back for dinner. The Saturday dinner was a club sponsored event and promised to be very entertaining. The hotel Banquet Room was reserved for club members and guests. It was an open bar, while the dinner was ala carte. You ordered from the menu at your expense.

We met Denise and Hank in the lobby and went into dinner

together, first stopping at the reception table, to pick up our name tags. Working the table was Tony. He smiled when he saw Hank and Hank, more civil after a nap and shower, smiled back.

The name tags were neatly printed in bold block letters and encased in a plastic holder with a pin back. Tony was handing them out as his escort, a very good looking blond, was checking off the names. *As Tony was handing out the tags, I noticed that he held them between his thumb and first finger. A perfect thumb print I thought, remembering my little task for Kaminski.* I took the tag and held it by it's edges, opened the pin back and slipped it into my lapel. Nobody paid any attention. They were all busy with their own tags.

I took Monica by the arm and we walked into the dining room, gravitating to the bar, with Hank and Denise following on our heels. There was a cocktail hour preceeding dinner. We stood around sipping our drinks, making small talk, and when a sufficient amout of time elapsed, about ten minutes, we headed for our table. On the way to the table I slipped off the name tag and stuck it in my pocket. When asked about it, I shrugged and laughed, *must have lost it, oh well you all know me.*

After dinner the entire group of diners were escorted into the Park, to the Western Saloon in Frontierland, where we all sang songs from printed song sheets, accompanied by a fiddler, a guitar and piano. We drank beer, sang, line danced and had an all around good time. The party broke up around 1:00 AM. It had been a full day, I was bushed and ready to hit the sack.

Sunday morning arrived at 8:00 AM. After breakfast we all headed over to the show area. A few straglers were still coming in, registration closed at 10:00 AM. Judging started at 11:00 AM. Before we walked the show area Hank gave his car a light dusting.

Hank was paying particular attention to his competition, his biggest worry was the Lago-Talbot. It was spectacular. When I commented on the car, he just grunted.

Judging was over by 2:00 PM, and the tabulation began. Hank was in class seven. We would have to wait until the awards banquet to find out the results. The competition was fierce. I was glad I did not bring the Merc. It was more fun just being a spectator, watching the others sweat.

Hank was extremely nervous, he hardly spoke, he kept going back to check the Lago-Talbot one more time. He intently watched the judges as they went over the Lago, then hurried back to his car, touched up a few things and waited to be judged. I thought it was a little comical, but Hank was dead serious.

The Sunday night Awards Banquet is a prepaid affair. Members prepay for dinner as part of the weekend registration package. As we sat down for the awards banquet, Hank had regained his confidence. He was all smiles and full of good cheer.

"Well how do you think it went?" I asked.

"What'ya mean?" He said.

"You know what I mean. How do you think the Mark did?"

"No problem. We did just fine. I just have to figure out where I'm going to put the damn trophy." He was really in good spirits.

"You're that sure. You know something we don't know."

"I watched them judge the Lago," He said. *I knew he figured the Lago was his biggest competition,* "He got knocked for his escutchen plates. They were a slightly pitted. He should have had them re-chromed like I did. This is a National, the car has got to be perfect, right?"

"Since you are that confident, I think this round should be on you."

"Hell, I'll do one better. I think Champagne is in order." He motioned for the waiter. "We'll have a bottle of Champagne and send one over to Valentines table. I think it's number five. It'll be his consolation prize."

"I take it you don't think Tony did very well."

"Are you kidding. With the Packard? Come on!"

"I thought it was a pretty nice car.." *I leaned back and watched Hank in all his glory, albeit a little premature.*

"Nice car, yes. But not a winner. Kind of like Tony you might say." *He was at it again, the cutting remarks. What the hell's got into him?*

All through dinner Hank was the life of the party. Our table saluted Tony's table and he acknowledged by sending over a bottle of Champagne, and saluted our table. We finally got settled down as the program moved into the awards presentation.

Since our chapter was the host chapter, and Hank was our president, he was required to give a little speech. It was short, he welcomed everyone and wished all the participants good luck.

After Hank's little speech, the head judge got up and went into the fine points of the awards program. The awards began with class one. When they got to class five, Tony's class, and announced that the third place award went to a 1941 Cadillac, owned by Tom Clark, Hank leaned over toward me and said, "see, nice car, but not a winner," referring to Tony's car. "The poor Bastard didn't even get third place."

I did not hear who got second place. When clapping finally settled down the judge went on to the next award. "And now for an outstanding classic, the first place award goes to none other than Tony Valentine, for his exceptional 1948 Packard Custom Eight."

Hank's mouth opened and nothing came out. He almost fell out of his chair. I got up and started clapping. Hank just glared. The expression on his face was priceless. We sat in silence through class six. When class seven was announced, Hank's class, he sat up straight, took a sip of Champagne, ran his hand through his hair, adjusted his tie and waited to be called to collect his prize.

Third place went to Al Flemming, who owned a really nice Logonda. Then the judge said, "it gives me great pleasure to make the next award. To an outstanding individual and I understand this is the first showing of this truly classic European design. I have not seen one any finer. Our second place winner, this one was close, for his 1950 Jaguar Mark V Drophead Coupe, Hank Palmer."

We all just sat there and looked at each other. I havn't been that uncomfortable in a long time. The clapping started, Hank got up and left the room. Denise finally got herself together, rose and received the award for Hank.

"I'll go see if I can find him." I said.

As I left the room first place was announced, John Henney's 1950 Lago-Talbot convertible. A very stunning car.

I found Hank sitting at the bar, and sat down next to him. I figured he did not want conversation, so I ordered a beer and we sat in silence.

After breakfast on Monday we loaded Hank's Jag onto an enclosed trailer and headed home. On the way Hank apologized for last night and nothing more was said on the subject. *Give him a couple of days, I thought, and he'll start planning for the next show.*

It was 11:30 AM when Hank dropped us off at the fire station. Monica and I lounged around most of the day. After lunch we went out for ice cream and then walked over to Edgewater Park to watch the fireworks.

CHAPTER 23

I hate long weekends, especially the working day after. Kaminski called me at 9:00 AM. I was preparing my final statement to the Kurtz's, for the loft job. The call broke my concentration, it was not welcome. I was somewhat curt on the phone, but we made arrangements to meet for lunch. At 10:00 AM my dad called, he had found another invoice. *Great!* I scrapped what I had complied so far and started over. At 11:00 AM Monica called to remind me about dinner with Mora. *Things were not going well, that's because it was a Tuesday/Monday. A Tuesday that should have been a Monday.*

Nothing goes right on Monday. Never buy a car made on Monday and never, never buy a car made on Tuesday following a holiday. By noon I gave up. *I'll work on this after lunch, I told myself.* I turned off the computer and went to meet Kaminski.

Kaminski's choice for lunch was Pier West, a posh restaurant located in one of the gold coast high rise buildings. *"Why does Kaminski always get to pick the restaurant", I muttered to myself, "and I always pick up the tab. What's wrong with this picture?"*

Dave Kaminski as usual, was on time. Dressed in a dark blue Armani subtle pinstripe, brilliant white shirt, understated print tie and black tasseled loafers. He carried himself with the demeanor of a successful attorney. I often told him he missed his calling, should have been prosecutor instead of a cop.

"Hi Noah, good to see you. Been waiting long?" He extended his hand as I rose.

"Not at all David. Not at all." We shook hands and sat down.

"So how was your weekend?" He asked. Picking up a menu. He never gave me a second glance before scanning the entries.

"My weekend was just fine Dave. And how was yours?"

"Super my friend. Super."

"Okay, okay, can we cut the polite shit and get to it."

"Fine with me." He put down the menu, smiling, "what have you got?"

I reached into the inside pocket of my jacket, retrieved an envelope and handed it to him. He took the envelope, looked inside at the plastic name tag, then looked at me.

"A perfect thumb print." I said. "Right hand." He closed the envelope, slipped it into his pocket and went back to the menu.

"That's it?" I said.

"What?" He raised his head from the menu. "You want a medal or something. For doing your civic duty, assisting law enforcement in a difficult case?"

"A simple, thank you would suffice."

"Thanks." He said with a little smile, and added, "nice job."

"You're welcome." I said picking up the menu.

We ordered lunch. Broiled trout, with wild rice. Dave was watching his weight.

After lunch, we relaxed over coffee and I prodded Dave about the case. "How is your investigation going?"

"Okay." He said, not wanting to give me anything more.

"You never did tell me who were the other suspected members

of the car club."

"It's confidential." He paused, "but since you stuck your neck out getting the print, I'll tell you. Strictly confidential" He added.

"Strictly confidential." I echoed.

"There are three," he said. "Valentine, Henney and Briggs. Each has purchased two or more cars out of Canada in the last ten months."

"Interesting," I said. "But just because they bought cars out of Canada doesn't make them bad guys."

"No it doesn't. But it's what ties them together and I believe proves out my theory of how the stuff is getting here." He took a sip of coffee. "They all altered there life styles in the last few months, somewhat drastically. Especially Valentine. He's the flamboyant one of the three. But we can tie Henney to the jeweler who's resetting the stones. If we can tie Valentine to the Preebe hit, I think he'll crack and implicate the others."

"Henney and Briggs are very respected, upstanding members of the community. Why would they get involved in such a scheme?"

"Don't know? But it probably has something to do with the money, you know the stuff that's the root of evil."

"What if the Valentine print doesn't match?"

"If we can't make Valentine, then it's back to more digging."

I wondered why Hank's name wasn't on the list. I knew he had acquired two cars in the last ten months. I knew the Mark V came out of Canada and I was pretty sure his XKE was from Toronto. I did not mention this to Dave, because I didn't think his theory held up.

We parted in the parking lot. "Take care of yourself Noah and thanks for this." He patted the breast pocket of his jacket.

"Just consider it my civic duty." I smiled. We shook hands and headed for our respective cars.

CHAPTER 24

I couldn't get Hank out of my mind. On my way back to the fire station I decided to call Denise. It rang three times before she picked up.

"Hi Denise, it's Noah."

"Hi Noah, what's up?" She was pretty chipper for a Tuesday/Monday.

"I was having a conversation this morning and Hank's XKE came up. Didn't he buy that in Toronto?"

"No, actually the car came from Toronto, but he bought it from John Henney."

"John Henney!"

"Yeah, isn't that wild and John beat Hank out at Pine Point. That's what set Hank off. Although for the life of me I don't know why. But then you know Hank. He's got to win. He's already planning for the Hershey show."

"That figures." I replied. "Thanks Denise, I'll talk to you later." I hung up and thought about Henney. *He sold a beautiful 1940 LaSalle to Myer Levy a few months back and the XKE to Hank, maybe he was making room for other cars? Maybe Dave did have something? Nah! Couldn't be. I just can't see it.* I curbed my thoughts and went back to work.

CHAPTER 25

At dinner Mora told us she spent the holiday weekend with her parents in Wisconsin. They wanted her to return, she told them she thought about it, but decided to stick around in Cleveland and try for a new beginning.

Speaking of beginnings, tomorrow, Wednesday, the salvage crew was scheduled to start their salvage operation of the Alice Good. Soon Mora would be very rich. When we asked her about her future plans, she simply shrugged and told us she wasn't really thinking about the money. The events of Sean's death were still fresh in her mind.

"How's your investigation going?" Mora asked.

"I'm going to take another shot at Mickey's boat. Right now it's all we have."

"What if you don't find the chart?" She asked.

"Then we'll just have to follow the gold. The missing gold bars from the Alice Good. Bullion is not that easy to dispose of. My friend Max has some connections, so we'll see." I sipped some coffee. "So, even if we don't come up with the chart we have other options."

"Noah you've done a lot already. Both of you." She looked over at Monica. "I don't want you to put yourself in any jeopardy. If something happened to you, and you got hurt I wouldn't be able to face myself, or Monica. You've already proved that it wasn't a burglary , that it was murder. We can go to the police with what you have and let them handle it."

"Mora, don't worry. I won't do anything stupid. I've come so far I'd like to see it through. If we can't do any better, then I'll go to the cops. That's a promise." I looked at her and Monica for approval. They both reluctantly agreed. The subject was closed.

CHAPTER 26

Wednesday at 8:00AM I got a call from Max. The lake was kicking up and it did not look promising for the salvage operation. He also told me that there was no activity at the dive site over the weekend. His feeling was that Mickey was backing off, undoubtedly accepting what he had recovered. He was going to cut and run, as Max put it. What he already recovered would make him a very wealthy man. So why not beat a retreat. It made good sense.

I told Max to hang around and see the salvage operation through. I would catch up with him later. After I hung up the salvage company called and confirmed that there would be no attempt made today. Tomorrow looked a lot better, but they would contact me in the morning to confirm. I gave them my cell phone number. I was going to try and hook up with Max later in the day.

I had a meeting with the Kurtz's at the loft at 10:00 AM, for a walk through and to present my final statement. I picked up a bottle of Champagne so we could celebrate. My dad would be there, Monica was still on vacation, so she agreed to be there. From there I planned to head for East Harbor, where Max could pick us up . Then we'd head back to Gull Island.

It was almost noon when we finally left the loft. The Kurtz's were very pleased and settled on the spot. I had a nice sizeable check tucked in my brief case. I decided to stop by the fire station and drop off the check. Monica waited in the car while I went up stairs. I put the check in the center drawer of my desk and was about to leave when I noticed the answering machine blinking. I was tempted to let it go but my curiosity got the better of me. The message was from Mora and I was to call her immediately.

"Mora, Noah. What's up?"

"You are not going to believe this." She was excited.

"What?" I asked.

"It's so strange." She said.

"What is?"

"Well," she started, "Mickey Kilbane called, no more than an hour ago, maybe less."

"What did he want?" I asked.

"Oh he didn't want anything, and this is the strange part, he just called to tell me he found this old chart on his boat and it looked a lot like the chart Sean had showed him. He didn't know how it got on his boat, but there it was. Did I want it?"

"You're kidding! What the hell kind of shit is this?" I was pacing around with the phone held tightly against my head.. Maybe I wasn't hearing this correctly. "He said what? Did he actually say it was Sean's chart? I can't believe this."

"I know", she said. "I couldn't believe it either."

"What did he actually say. I mean his actual words."

"He said he went down to his boat early this morning to try and get in some fishing. The lake was acting up so he scraped the idea of fishing and decided to do some house cleaning instead. In the side pocket on the bridge he found the old chart. It was sticking up in the pocket. It didn't look right, he pulled it out and it immediately struck him that it looked very much like the chart Sean showed him, right down to the pencil marks."

"What the hell was he trying to pull? It's probably the chart alright. But why call you? Why tell you he has it? It's some kind of ruse. He knows we are on to him and he's trying to cover his ass. Slick bastard."

"What should I do? She asked.

"How did you leave it with him?"

"That I wasn't sure I wanted it."

"Good. Just sit tight. I'll get back to you when I figure this out. And by the way I got a call from the salvage people it's not going to be today. Maybe tomorrow. I'll keep you posted, In the mean time you've got my cell number, if anything else comes up call me on the cell."

What the hell kind of a game was Mickey playing? Come on Noah, you're a bright boy, reason this out. My mind was not working. I went down stairs to join Monica. I told her about Mora's call, she thought that maybe Mickey was innocent. Maybe I was crowding myself, I should just sit back and take an objective look. *Maybe she was right, I thought about it for the couple of hours it took to drive out to East Harbor.*

Max picked us up with his boat and we headed for Gull Island. The lake was a little choppy, waves were two to four feet. It wasn't something Max's boat couldn't handle, but the ride past Kellys Island was a little bouncy. The jarring ride and the lake spray did have it's effect, I did start to think more clearly. *Maybe Monica was right and I just couldn't see it. What if Mickey was innocent. What then? Who then? Who elso knew of the charts significance? There was one obvious choice, but murder just did not factor into it.*

About 4:00 PM the wind subsided and the lake began to settle down. We were relaxing on the porch of the cottage, drinking beer and snacking on chips and pretzels, listening to Max's golden oldies station. I picked up the field glasses and surveyed the dive site for the third time.

"See anything?" Asked Max, also for the third time.

"Just water, just water. Oh wait, here comes a visitor." I adjusted the glasses trying to focus a littler better.

"Anyone we know?" Pipped Max trying to be humorous.

"Let's see. A little to far away but the heading is in this general direction."

"Let me have a look." Max said reaching for the glasses.
"Well it's a Bayliner, blue over white. Really pouring it on."

"May I take a look", Asked Monica. Max handed her the glasses.

"I don't see a boat."

"To your left", instructed Max.

"Yes. Now I see it, a blue and white boat. I see one person. But I cannot tell if it is a man or women." She continued to follow the approaching boat. "It appears to be slowing down."

"Yeah, looks that way." Max and I were observing without the benefit of the glasses, but you could see the boat was reducing power.

"I still can not see who is at the wheel," she said.

"Got to be a man." I said.

"What?" Asked Monica.

"I said, it's got to be a man."

"It looks like a man." She said.

"I would have to agree." Said eagle eye Max, looking out over the water shading his eyes.

The boat slowed and came to a stop over the dive site. The figure on board cut power and lowered the anchor, Then he went below. Monica lowered the glasses and relinquished them to me. I took them and fixed on the anchored Bayliner. As the figure emerged from the cabin dressed in a diving suit he turned toward Gull Island, then bent down picked something up and went back in the cabin.

"Shit!" I said pretty much to myself but loud enough for Max to hear as I handed him the glasses.

"Where are you going?" Asked Monica.

"Out to that boat." I said running down to the dock as fast as I could.

"But why?" Monica words trailed behind me.

I reached the dock and untied the dingy. One pull of the outboard starter cord and the twenty-five horsepower motor came to life. I gave the tiller a sharp yank to the right and headed straight for the dive site.

I approached the anchored boat from the bow, hoping to make my appearance as much of a surprise as possible. I knew he would hear the high whine of the dingy, but he couldn't see me. I was hoping he would think it was a passing fisherman. At the last minute I cut the motor, whipped the dingy into a hard left, came up on his blind side and drifted up to the swim platform. I lashed the dingy to the swim platform and eased myself up onto the platform. The boat rocked under my weight. So much for surprises.

Max continued to monitor the situation from the island. He had the field glasses trained on the deck of the Bayliner, with Monica continually asking for a play by play.

The figure of a man emerged from the cabin dressed in a dive suit, a face mask sitting atop his head.

"Nice day for a dive don't you think Noah?"

"I don't know Hank, I've seen better."

"Hey sometimes we can't be picky. We got to take what we can get. You know how it is."

"One question Hank, why?"

"What'ya mean?"

"Cut the shit Hank. Why did you kill Sean?"

"If I told you it was an accident, would you believe me?"

"Try me." I said, keeping my sea legs, steadying myself against the rocking boat.

"He wouldn't listen to reason. He was screwing things up. I was being squeezed out of a good thing because Sean got cold feet. He told me about the chart and how he figured out about the gold. He said there was enough for both of us. We could be partners. We didn't need the other stuff, it was over for him. I told him he was fantasizing. He kept saying no, no, we could be rich. He was done and that was it. I said he was crazy. He grabbed the map and came at me. I gave him a shove, he lost his balance, fell and hit the back of his head on the fireplace mantel."

"Why didn't you just call the police. It was an accident, you didn't have to run."

"See, I told you, you wouldn't understand. I couldn't do that, it would screw things up. So I took the chart and his notebook and made it look like a burglary. Everything was fine until you came nosing around. Didn't you go back to Mickey's boat? Didn't you find the stupid chart there?"

"Hank you have to turn yourself in. It's your only chance,"

"Too late ole' buddy. Things have gone to far. No turning back now."

Max dropped the glasses, grabbed Monica by the hand and jerked her toward the dock. She almost fell, stumbling along, as he ran to the dock.

"Max, what is wrong?" She gasped.

"We need to get to the boat and fast." Max jumped from the dock on to the 'Columbine'. As Monica untied the lines Max fired up the boat. Then he gave it full throttle and headed straight for the Bayliner. They were halfway there when they heard the shot.

Hank's hand came from behind his back. He was holding a nine millimeter Beretta and pointed it right at me. I was startled and nearly lost my footing. My knees got a little weak. He had a desperate look in his eyes. He was only six feet away and couldn't miss.

"Hank, this is a mistake. You're not a killer, put the gun down. I'll go to the cops with you."

I didn't hear a sound, only saw the flash, and felt the deep burning sensation, as I tumbled backwards into the water. The darkness closed in, I felt nothing else. Soldiers in combat will tell you, that you never hear the one that gets you. No sound, only the feeling. I never thought it would end like this.

CHAPTER 27

When I opened my eyes I was no longer in the water. I was strapped to a gurney in the back of an ambulance. Monica was there holding my hand and sirens were screaming. I closed my eyes and the blackness took over.

When I finally regained full consciousness I was in a bed, covered with crisp sheets and a light blanket. My shoulder was in a cast supported by a rod attached to a partial body cast. There were some flowers in the room and the sun was shining outside my window. Monica was smiling down at me, she put her hand to my face.

"How are you feeling?"

"Sore. Numb." I continued to look around, "where am I?"

"Port Clinton Hospital."

"How long have I been here?"

"Two days."

"Hank, what about Hank?"

"Everything is okay." She held my free hand.

"But what happened? I remember the gun, falling in the water. What happp……. " I was cut off when the door opened and Max entered the room.

"How you doing kiddo? I told you not to grandstand. No percentage in it. Got to know when to pull the plug, otherwise shit happens, people get hurt." Max had a big smile on his face, he approached my good side and put a hand on my shoulder, "You done good."

"But what happened? Will somebody please fill me in."

Max looked at Monica, "I guess we better fill him in, he's getting a little testy." Monica nodded and smiled, deferring to Max.

"First off, just before Hank pulled the trigger, Monica and I started for the dive site, we were halfway there when we heard the shot and saw you go into the drink. Hank saw us coming and fired up his boat. Monica dove in about where you hit the water, I went after Hank. The dingy tied to the swim platform slowed him down, and then the dingy tie line fouled his prop and he was dead in the water. I figured he wasn't going anywhere so I came about, called the Coast Guard, which in turn contacted Kaminski. By that time Monica here, had you up to the surface, we hauled you aboard the 'Columbine" and made a straight shot for the mainline. The Coast Guard picked up our boy Henry. End of story. The rest you'll have to get from your friend Kaminski."

"When I saw the gun I didn't think Hank would shot." I said

"He was scared, cornered, it was a reflex. I don't think he really thought it through." Replied Max.

"You're probably right." I said.

"Right now I'm on my way to wrap up the salvage operation.

They recovered seventy-five of the bars, estimated worth over fifteen million dollars. The State of Ohio boys were on hand and chopping at the bit, they will no doubt take a hefty chunk." Said Max.

"Only seventy-five bars? I thought the original cargo was one hundred bars."

"I wondered about that. Someone else may have found the site or there never were one hundred bars. We'll never know." He gave me a little salute and departed.

"Max was wonderful." Said Monica. "He new exactly what to do and there was no nonsense."

"How about you?" I said. "Sounds like you were pretty wonderful."

She leaned over and kissed me long and hard. "Now get some rest, the doctor said you will be going home tomorrow."

She squeezed my hand and turned to leave. At the door she stopped and turned, "Mora called, she would like to see us, once you are settled in at home. I told her we would call. The flowers are from her, the card is on the side table next to you." She blew me a kiss and left.

I picked up the card. On the front was a picture of a knight dressed in armor, sitting atop a white horse. I opened it. It read, *How can I ever thank you. Get well, see you soon. Love Mora.*

Later that day my folks stopped by, my dad said he was glad I was okay, but that I should learn to duck and stop playing detective. "Stick to renovating." Were his words. After they left, I finally got some sleep.

CHAPTER 28

I was no sooner settled in at the fire station when Kaminski called, He was coming over at 3:00 PM. On hearing this Monica went out to Geschke's Bakery on Madison and picked up a strudel. It's what you do when you have guest's in the afternoon.

If you got points for promptness Dave Kaminski would be the winner, hands down. Exactly at 3:00 PM the buzzer at the street door sounded. Monica let him in and waited to greet him at the head of the stairs.

"Hello", she said, I'm Monica, and you must be Noah's friend David. It's nice to finally meet you." She extended her hand.

"The pleasure, I assure you, is all mine." Smiling as he took her hand. Dave was all charm and smiles as he entered the apartment. I rose form my chair and met him halfway.

"Hi Dave glad you could stop by, " I extended my good hand.

"Hi Noah, you look great in the mummy get up. How are you doing?"

"Very funny. I'm doing great. Come on over and sit down." He took one of the arm chairs facing the couch. Monica and I sat on the couch.

"To what do we owe the pleasure of this visit. It's not official, is it?" I was trying to be funny.

"No. Nothing like that I just wanted to see how you were getting along."

"You could have gotten that on the phone. So what's up?"

"The truth is, I owed you one. I thought I'd like to fill you in before you started asking questions."

"Thanks, and you don't owe me. But I would like to know what happened."

"What do you know so far?" He asked.

I started to answer when Monica interrupted, "Before you get started, would you like something to drink? Coffee, or something cold?"

"Something cold would be fine." He said.

"Now do not start till I get back." She instructed.

Monica returned in a few minutes with a tray of iced tea and strudel. She set it down on the coffee table.

"This looks great," remarked Dave reaching for a slice of

strudel. "Home made?" He asked.

"Yes, but not by me. Now you can start."

Dave went on to tell us about the theft ring. The head and mastermind of the ring was Alexander Kent. "Does that ring a bell?" He asked.

"Yes, I remember Alex, he used to be president of our club chapter. As I recall he moved to England, or was transferred there."

"Right," continued Dave. "Kent was the one who arranged to have the stolen European jewelry shipped to Canada. He came up with the scheme of removing the stones and melting down the settings. Making it very difficult to trace. And then resetting the stones and selling them as estate jewelry. Henney was the one who thought of moving the stones in antique cars. If we hadn't received a tip from the jeweler resetting the stones, we never would have gotten Henney. And of course the Classic Car Owners Club gave us the tie-in to the others."

"So the club was your common denominator?"

"Right. We figured that three members were involved initially, but after we arrested Valentine, thanks to your good work, he implicated your friend Hank, who in turn recruited Sean Kilbane as a pawn."

"So Hank was in on the scheme."

"Right. He was in on the scheme from the beginning."

"I am not sure I understand. What part did Sean play?" Asked Monica.

"Henney and Briggs were getting a little nervous. The stones had been coming across from Canada by boat, but the Coast Guard began to tighten that up, so they switched to cars. They needed someone to drive the cars from Buffalo to Cleveland. That's where Sean came into the picture. He did business in Buffalo and he needed the money. But he apparently got cold feet after a couple of runs. So after he found the chart and figured out the Alice Good connection to the gold, he wanted out. Hank panicked, he was getting pressure from Henney and Briggs. So he confronted Sean, they struggled and Sean was accidentally killed."

"So it was an accident." I said.

"So it seems, the Lakewood cops are still putting things together. But I'm afraid your friend Hank is going to do some time."

"Poor Hank. What I don't understand is why Hank would have gotten involved in the first place?"

"Greed. Money. Same old stuff. He was supporting a habit. Not a drug habit, but an antique car habit. Henry Palmer wanted to own Classic Cars that he really could not afford. He was dipping into his bank and covering the withdrawals with his share of the jewelry money. They were hauling in a lot of money. A couple of more shipments and he wouldn't need the bank anymore. All this was before he found out about the gold. By then it was to late."

"What about Chuck Preebe? Who killed him?" I asked.

"According to Valentine, it was Henney who pulled the trigger. So Henney is up for Murder two, with Valentine as an accomplice

218

and Briggs gets nailed with grand theft."

"Unbelievable!" I slumped back. "And what about you, where do you go from here?"

"Me, I'm back at my old desk in Homicide." He got to his feet, "and this is where I exit."

"Thanks for coming over, and thanks for filling us in. We have got to get together one of these days, you and Kathy, Monica and I. Go out for dinner or something."

"That would be nice." He said.

"I'll call your wife," volunteered Monica, "we will make all the arrangements."

Monica and I watched as Dave descended the stairs, it was almost 5:00 PM and we were going over to Mora's for dinner.

CHAPTER 29

We arrived at Mora's at 6:30 PM. All through dinner Mora was behaving like the proverbial cat that swallowed the canary.

In the final settlement, the State of Ohio took their percentage and after taxes, Mora was left with over four and a half million dollars, free and clear. The gold was classified as industrial grade, so the value was calculated at a little less than market. She wasn't sure what she would do with the money, but it would help her get a new start. She deserved it.

After dinner we relaxed in the living room drinking coffee, and in my case sipping beer. We were all settled and comfortable when she dropped her bomb. She left the room and returned in a few seconds holding a piece of paper in her hand, which she handed to me.

"What's this?"

"It's a check." She said.

"Yes I can see that, but why, what for?" I held the check in my hand so Monica could see it. It was for four hundred seventy-eight thousand dollars.

"I don't understand?"

"It's your fee." She said sipping her coffee, a big smile on her face.

"My fee?" Now look Mora, I can't except this."

"Why not? It's your standard fee for recovery. I checked."

"What!" I looked at Monica, she turned away. I knew it, these two have been talking.

"I insist that you take it. You earned it. Remember we had a deal, it was a professional arrangement. And we Kilbanes' always pay our debts." There was no arguing with her. So I folded the

220

check and put it in my pocket.

"Thanks very much, " I said, "very generous. And speaking of Kilbanes', I guess I owe Mickey an apology."

"He called today, invited me on his boat this weekend."

"What did you say?" Asked Monica.

"I told him I'd think about it."

"Go." Said Monica. "You need to get out."

On the way home I told Monica that I would make sure Max got a share of the check. She told me not too. "Remember the bar we retrieved? Well Mora told him to keep it."

"Really! Good for Max, he earned it."

I leaned back in the passenger seat, thinking about what to do with the money. *There was this fifteen room Victorian house that Monica and I were interested in. It needed a little work, but sat on two acres of beautiful, prime land, outside of Medina. We could swing it without a mortgage, fix it and flip it. But the thing is, there was this 1956 Porsche 356C that just came on the market. It was red, tan top and saddle leather interior, fully restored. And the price was right. Priorities! It's all about priorities! What's a guy to do?*

Don Narus, is a retired entrepreneur, an automotive historian and Korean War veteran. He has written four Automotive History books and two Mystery novels. He and his wife Lee live in New Albany, Ohio where he is working on his next mystery novel.

This book and previous books can be purchased on Amazon.com or LuLu.com.
Also by the author:
"Chryslers Wonderful Woodie-The Town and Country"
    Vol. 1 and Vol.2
"Great American Woodies and Wagons"
"Steering Wheels and Dashboards-1939-1949"
"Apparent Suicide"
"Cruise To Die For"

Authors Notes:

A number of ship wrecks can be found in the Great Lakes. Some of these wrecks have only been recently found. One such ship was found in August of 2007. The Cyprus, an ore freighter, that mysteriously sank two months after it was launched. All but one of the crew had perished on October 11, 1907. The story of The Cyprus led to the story of the Alice Good.

There are between 15,00 and 3,00 sunken ships in the Great Lakes. Only about 400 have been found and not all have been identified.

For more information on sunken ships in the Great Lakes, visit the Maritime Archives at Bowling Green University, Bowling Green, Ohio, or check the Great Lakes Sunken Ships on line. Also there are a number of books on the subject which can be found at Amazon.com or your local library.